TEXAS COWBOY'S FAMILY

BARB HAN

TORJAKE PUBLISHING

Copyright © 2019 by Barb Han

All rights reserved.

No part of this book may be reproduced in any form or by any electronic or mechanical means, including information storage and retrieval systems, without written permission from the author, except for the use of brief quotations in a book review.

Editing: Ali Williams

Cover Design: Jacob's Cover Designs

To my family for unwavering love and support. I can't imagine doing life with anyone else.

1

"Take her. Keep her safe."

Emery Young had been half-asleep when her sister had dropped off Aria in the middle of the night. All Emery remembered clearly from the visit was that Haven had moved the new portable crib she'd brought over a few days ago next to the bed and then gently placed her six-week-old daughter inside. It should have struck Emery as odd except that Haven had been talking about doing a drop off for the past few days, saying she needed just one morning to sleep in.

The sun wasn't due to rise for another hour when a noise woke Emery. Aria was probably stirring. She would be hungry. As Emery stumbled out of the bed to search around for her niece's diaper bag, the first hint that something might be seriously wrong hit her.

A note was sitting on top of the bag. Emery blinked her eyes a couple of times as she reached for the light switch on the nightstand. She suppressed a yawn as she picked up the paper and held it to the light. Reading the words had the effect of a double shot of espresso.

If you don't hear from me in the next hour, take the baby and hide. Please. Don't tell anyone and don't go to the police.

The police? Why would she go to the cops?

Emery immediately ran to her dresser where her smartphone sat on its charger. Instead of hers, she found a temporary one and another note. *I'll explain later. Keep this with you at all times.*

It was then Emery realized it hadn't been her niece who had caused her to wake. An alarm had been set on the new phone and it was going off again.

Emery picked it up and squinted at the screen, her eyes still blurry from sleep, or lack of it. Working as a night nurse at a home for senior living while taking classes for her nursing degree left little room for much else, including rest.

All it took was a fingertip to the screen to stop the alarm from sounding. However, the one inside her head screeched even louder after reading the label: *Go. Hide. Now.*

Emery searched her thoughts for recent signs of distress from Haven and came up empty. Her sister had given zero indication that anything was wrong, let alone anything that would qualify as an emergency. This whole scenario ending up a bad joke was out of the question. Her sister wasn't the dramatic type and would never pull a prank like this—this would just be cruel. Haven was also the person who dotted every I and crossed every T.

A feeling deep in the pit of Emery's stomach surfaced, telling her something was very wrong. She unplugged the new cell phone and tucked it along with its cord into the diaper bag. She brushed her teeth and then pulled her hair back, wrangling it into a ponytail before grabbing her weekend bag. Next, she grabbed undergarments, jeans, and a few shirts along with her small travel bag filled with toiletries.

There was enough to get her through a couple of days by the time she finished packing. She refused to think she'd need more than that. The thought anything serious could happen to her sister was so far out of the realm of possibility that Emery tucked the notion away.

Whatever was going on, Haven would come home, explain everything and life as normal could resume. Thankfully, Emery was on summer break from her studies, so she could afford to keep a low profile until everything was set right. She worked four days on and three off, so she was clear there, too.

Lifting Aria, Emery took note that her niece's

diaper was still fresh before placing the little girl inside a carrier that doubled as a car seat. Next, she ran out to her car and put the weekend and diaper bag in the back seat. Another trip and the portable crib was secured in her vehicle.

Carefully scanning the area, a chill raced up her spine that someone could be out there watching. She dashed back inside her apartment for the baby carrier and her purse. She'd always had a good imagination and it was running wild.

At this time of the morning, there wasn't usually a person in sight let alone a car moving in the lot. When a noise sounded to her right in the landscaping, she nearly jumped out of her skin. Quietly, she took a couple of steps closer to get a look. A raccoon came waddling out of the bushes, barely regarding her as it kept moving.

Adrenaline pumped through Emery's body and the jolt of energy that came with it had her wide-awake despite the early hour. She had never been nor would ever be considered a morning person. To her, this time was still considered the middle of the night.

As she secured baby Aria in the backseat, the hairs on the back of her neck pricked. She wrote the creepy feeling off as her nerves. Morning thunder rumbled in the distance. The sky was filled with clouds so thick they blanketed the sky. The starless night made it seem even darker out. Normally, that would bother her. Not tonight. She appreciated the darkness.

Gripping the steering wheel, she turned the key in the ignition and said a prayer her car would start. Thankfully, her car started. It had been making a strange noise lately and she'd been needing to take it to the shop. It was then that she noticed how much her hands were shaking.

Emery told herself that Haven was fine, and all of this could somehow easily be explained, despite the scary scenarios running through her mind. At least, to Emery's thinking, there was no way her sister could have done anything wrong. She was the most straight-and-narrow person on earth. If anyone was going to get into trouble between the two sisters, it would've been Emery. After all, she'd been the rebellious one growing up. She'd been the one to run off with her musician boyfriend within an hour of high school graduation. She'd toured the country first in his pickup and then an RV as his band's popularity grew.

Haven made everyone's life easier. She used to get up early to make Emery's lunch while their single mother worked all night at the hospital. Haven had been the one to get a part-time job once she turned sixteen, to help their mother buy a newer car so the two of them could share. She'd been the one to make perfect grades whereas Emery struggled in school, still did. And Haven had been the one to move back home to drive their mother to all her doctor appointments when she'd become suddenly and deathly ill.

Emery had volunteered to quit her job and move in with their mother, but Haven had argued that she was already there and wanted Emery to keep her life as normal as possible. Days later, her mother had passed away while Emery was making the drive to Fort Worth from Austin. She mentally shook off memories and refocused on her current situation as she pulled out of her apartment complex.

Turning onto Chestnut Avenue, heading toward the highway, she passed a slow-moving vehicle. The black truck had temporary license plates, blacked-out windows and cruised way below the speed limit.

Since most Texans kept a heavy foot on the gas pedal, it struck her as odd. The vehicle was coming toward her on the two-lane road. *It's probably nothing*, she told herself. She was being paranoid and her senses here on high alert.

The truck slowed even more as it approached. A fresh shot of adrenaline had her ducking down so the driver couldn't get a good look at her face.

Heart pounding her rib cage, she kept a low profile as she picked up speed. Through the sideview mirror she saw the truck U-turn. Warning sirens sounded inside her head. Instinct took over. She floored the gas pedal.

It was early morning and no one else was around.

She didn't have a plan. And the truck was gaining on her.

The lack of cars and people on the road worked against her. It was unlikely she would see anyone until she got out of her neighborhood and onto a new road. She needed to think of where to go. And fast.

There was the main drag where people would be out and about or the highway. It was possible she could lose the truck in one of those places. People would be starting their day.

High beams flipped on, blinding her with light. She blinked, trying to focus. It was impossible to see the driver as the truck caught up to her. He was on her tail now and it was only a matter of time before he tapped her bumper.

One word came to mind. *Cops*. Her sister had said no police. Haven couldn't possibly have known Aria's and Emery's lives would be in danger. The police station was four blocks away. She had to try to make it before this guy slammed into her back bumper and sent her into a tailspin. At this rate, it wouldn't take long and she was surprised he hadn't nailed her already.

Pushing her hatchback as fast as it would go, she hit a hard brake before making a quick right. The dual spotlights on her tracked her like a bloodhound hot on a scent.

This time, Aria stirred for real. She belted out a

scream from the backseat that nearly cracked Emery's heart in two. For a six-week-old infant, the girl had a set of pipes on her that could rival a serial killer victim in a B-rated movie.

The truck crossed into the oncoming lane and tried to overtake her. Emery had to think fast. She wheeled the steering wheel left, blocking the maneuver. She cringed, waiting for the hit to her back bumper.

In a surprising move, the truck slowed down and settled in behind her. The high beams bounced off her rearview mirror, hit her square in the eyes and straight through her skull, guaranteed to bring on a migraine.

No way would Emery allow this jerk to run her off the road. Were it not for Aria in the backseat, she would stop right then and there to confront them. Under the circumstances, that would be irresponsible and dangerous. Emery had no idea what this person was capable of or what his involvement could be with her sister's situation. Being asked to steer clear of the cops and go into hiding without an explanation put Emery at a severe disadvantage.

Did this guy know where Haven was? Her sister could have gone into hiding, figuring her daughter would be safer with Emery.

Her grip tightened around the steering wheel. One more block and she would be home free. There was no doubt in her mind the truck wouldn't follow her into the police station parking lot.

Then, the second surprising move happened. The driver cut down his lights and slowed. Did he realize she was driving him straight into a trap?

With the breathing room she needed, she easily swerved into the lot and maneuvered as close to the front door as possible. She debated going into the station and asking for help. But what kind of help would she be asking for exactly?

Any officer on duty would most likely look at her like she was crazy if she tried to explain what had happened, what *was* happening, without bringing her sister into the equation.

Emery surveyed the area, the stillness of the parking lot in stark contrast to the heavy winds now shaking the car. She said soothing words to Aria, who was quietly crying but could hear the tension in her own voice.

A storm was kicking up as the first droplets of rain pelted her windshield. There was no sign of the truck, which didn't mean it wasn't lurking around somewhere. This was the exact situation or kind of situation that would have Emery reaching out to her big sister for advice. Her brain still couldn't fathom the fact that Haven could be in real trouble except that the truck had brought the danger to Emery's doorstep.

What if she'd stayed in her apartment five minutes longer? A shiver raced down her back right before the firebolt came. Anger fired through her veins as she thought about the driver taking Aria. Emery would've fought back.

The idea that the truck might've shown up because something had happened to Haven was a gut punch.

No. Impossible. Haven would call, she decided, canceling out all other possibilities. Haven would probably reach out in the next hour and clear this whole situation up. It was probably just a misunderstanding anyway. Who could want to hurt her sister? There was no father in the picture since Aria was conceived via in vitro. She was not only smart but kind and giving. She worked hard. Emery couldn't remember a time when anyone had said harsh words about her sister.

Since the truck hadn't resurfaced and the baby needed soothing, Emery decided it was safe to make her move. She put the gearshift into drive and eased out of the parking lot.

Certain that she wasn't being followed and no longer able to stomach hearing her sweet little niece cry in the backseat, Emery pulled into the first roadside gas station that operated twenty-four hours and parked.

The massive convenience store near the highway was a beacon to the slogan that everything was bigger in Texas. This place had everything from freshly-cooked meals to souvenirs to all the convenience items a person could want for a road trip. Beef

Jerky? Check. Fountain drinks? Yes. Corn chips? Definitely.

"Hold on, sweet girl. I bet it's time for you to eat." Emery had changed her fair share diapers in the six weeks since her niece had been born. She'd helped her sister with feedings, too, spending more time at Haven's townhouse than she had at her own apartment.

Summer was perfect timing for Haven to give birth for Emery to be available to pitch in. Having Aria on her own had been Haven's decision. She'd decided that by thirty she was going to start her family with or without a spouse. Emery suspected that her sister's timeline had become even more important after the heartbreak at being left at the altar two years ago.

Emery had no such timeline for her own life. Her hands were full taking care of herself and she was just now starting to get her footing after spending five years on the road with an up-and-coming band. Her boyfriend started hitting the jazz charts and decided to relocate to New Orleans. Emery was Texan through-and-through. No way she was moving out of state.

As much as she'd wandered, she never lost sight of who she was. Touring full-time with his band for years to come had been about as appealing as living in New Orleans by herself, waiting for her beau to have a break in his schedule to come home. No thanks.

If Haven had been voted most likely to succeed in

high school, Emery had been voted least likely to start a family. The traditional life with two-point-five kids, a husband, and a minivan had never held any appeal. And she could admit that even after settling down in Fort Worth for the past two years and working toward her nursing degree, the itch to get up and go had grown with each passing month.

With some effort, Emery managed to grab a bottle and supplies while balancing the baby carrier on one arm. She located a store worker, whose smile and sunny disposition would normally cause Emery to smile back. A crying child who desperately needed soothing only brought on more of that feeling of panic.

"Let me help you with that." The worker mixed a bottle and heated the water, testing it on the inside of her wrist. With an equally big smile, she handed over the baby's meal.

"Thank you." Those two words barely made a dent in expressing the well of gratitude she felt. Emery wasn't sure what she would've done without assistance in warming Aria's bottle.

Returning to the safety of her car, she settled Aria with a meal before changing the little girl's diaper. A thought struck. Where should she go now?

Get on the road and drive. Austin was the best place to find shelter. She'd been friendly with club owners and managers and it would be easy to find a crash pad there. Once that was settled, Emery got back on the road and headed south.

A few hours of silence passed before Aria stirred again. Her cries started out small, building to an intense crescendo.

Stopping in the little town of Gunner hadn't been part of the plan until Aria's screams reached a fever pitch. It was then that Emery realized she'd forgotten to burp the little girl. Gas pain was most likely the cause of her niece's discomfort. A stab of physical pain struck in the realization that Emery had forgotten something so basic.

Her stomach growled, reminding her that she hadn't had breakfast. Or coffee. No caffeine did bad things to her brain. She could only hope the small town had a place for her to eat. At least the sun was up and the threat of rain had dwindled.

Driving through the town square, she made note of the fact that it was early on a Sunday morning. In her hometown of Fort Worth, that would mean quiet streets. Here, she took note of the handful of trucks parked near a bakery. There was an inn next door and a moment of inspiration struck. Maybe she wouldn't have to go all the way to Austin.

Emery tried to soothe the crying baby by singing a lullaby. On the road with her ex-boyfriend's band, The Smooth Texas Seven, she'd sung backup a time or two when needed. Emery figured her voice wasn't awful.

But Aria was having none of it. In fact, she seemed to scream louder. Emery skimmed the landscape. The park across the street would give her a chance to stretch her legs and hopefully some fresh air would do the baby good.

Eyeing the streets carefully, she could only hope the area was safe.

2

By the time Emery parked and freed Aria from the constraints of the car seat, her own nerves were on edge. "You're okay, sweet girl. I'm here. And your mom is going to call any minute to tell us where to meet her."

Emery had no idea if Aria was old enough to notice that her mom was gone. Based on her fussiness, Emery thought maybe so. Ten pounds had never felt so heavy than when little Aria was crying. It literally ripped Emery's heart out of her chest not to be able to provide comfort to the little angel. Aria was a good baby and didn't normally fuss unless it was to let them know she was hungry or needed a diaper change.

After tucking the temporary cell phone in her pocket followed by her car key, Emery set out to walk around the playground as desperation started to sink in. She couldn't go there, couldn't go to the place in her mind where her sister was anything but all right. The alternative was unthinkable.

Not being able to calm Aria wasn't exactly providing a confidence boost. Emery made another lap around the swings, thinking how much she'd loved to swing when she was a little girl.

The more Aria cried, the more crushing helplessness enveloped Emery. Nothing had ever made her feel so helpless. And that was saying a lot. Emery didn't do helpless. The word had not entered her vocabulary until now.

She'd only been left alone with Aria long enough for her sister to make a grocery run or take a quick shower. Haven had always timed their alone time to right after feedings when Aria was conked out and all Emery had to do was rock the little girl in her arms and marvel at how tiny and beautiful she was.

For a split second, Emery considered driving back to the Fort Worth police station and bringing in the law to help find her sister. She reminded herself this whole ordeal would be over by dinner. Her sister would make contact and Emery and Aria would be on the road in no time. No harm. No foul. The notion that Haven might not call was so unfathomable that Emery couldn't even go there hypothetically.

Emery made a gentle bouncing motion in another attempt to calm Aria. Again, her niece wasn't having it.

How could something so tiny make so much noise or make Emery's heart hurt so much? The dark clouds that had been hanging overhead felt like a weighted blanket around Emery's shoulders.

In a desperate moment, she glanced around looking for someone who had more experience with babies than her, which wouldn't take much. There was no one at the park this early. Emery tilted Aria up and gently patted her back, trying to ease some of the gas pain.

In her nurse's training, she'd learned how important good communication with her patients was in being able to pinpoint what was really going on. Not being able to ask Aria why she was crying and if she was in any pain put Emery at a disadvantage. Understanding a patient's need was at the core of providing good care.

Emery hummed another lullaby as she patted little Aria's back. Being out in the open wasn't ideal and she could only hope her car would start again when it was time to go. Gently bouncing up and down, frustration built when Emery felt like she was only making things worse for Aria.

And when Emery was out of ideas to calm her niece, she joined her. Emery stopped fighting the tears that had been threatening to fall since this whole ordeal had started.

Still, none came.

ELI QUINN HAD TUCKED the invitation to his brother's wedding into his nightstand before heading downtown and to the playground with his kids. He had no qualms about attending Aiden and Chloe's wedding next month. In fact, six of his brothers had found the happiness with a partner that Eli hadn't been able to give his ex-wife, Camille.

The Fort Worth socialite had convinced him that she'd had fallen in love with the ranch, with all things country, and with him. He'd gone all-in. Hook, line, and sinker. They'd had two children together after a whirlwind courtship before she decided she didn't love him anymore and couldn't handle ranch life. Their entire relationship had played out in three short and packed years.

He'd been a sucker, too, because he loved his wife. He'd done his level best to make her happy and his ego was still bruised from the failure. At least he got the two most amazing kids in the world out of the deal. Camille had walked away from Oliver and Olivia without so much as a backward glance, giving him full custody and requesting zero visitation.

Trying to figure out how he'd let himself fall for someone who didn't return the sentiment or could be so indifferent toward her own kids had been an exercise in futility. Eli had miscalculated. It wasn't the kind of mistake he normally made.

Licking his wounds would do no good. Eli had decided a long time ago that life was a lot like using a car's navigation system; there were times when directions were misleading, and he took a wrong turn. On the road, he was able to correct his mistake and get back on course, smarter. Life wasn't much different.

Committing to a path had been the missing piece in Camille. She wasn't the settling down type. Last he'd heard, she moved onto an oil tycoon in Houston where she currently lived. Eli figured the relationship would play out in a similar fashion. Camille wasn't the kind of person who could settle in for the long haul; Eli's only regret was that he'd cost his children a mother by not realizing it sooner.

The situation was a catch-22. Without question, Eli would trade his life for his kiddos. Blessed didn't begin to describe how he felt with those two angels in his life. Not being able to give them a mother at all, let alone one they deserved, would always be a knife to the chest —and history repeating itself?

As Eli pushed his little girl on the swing at the downtown Gunner playground, he could only hope he would be enough for her and her brother. Dating wasn't his priority. The thought of bringing another person into their world who could turn tail and walk out again wasn't even a consideration. Between rising at four a.m. for ranch work and taking care of Oliver and Olivia, he didn't have much energy left for dating anyway.

So, he was caught off guard when a stray lightning bolt struck his chest the minute he caught sight of a stranger holding an infant in her arms while walking up the jogging path. He didn't want to notice her heart-shaped face, or how shiny her blacker-than-the-night-sky hair was as the clouds scattered and sunbeams reflected off it. Her fashionable ripped jeans didn't exactly scream stability. Even though he didn't get off the ranch much, it was easy to see she was new in town and most likely passing through.

Chin to chest, he also realized she was trying to hide the fact she was crying as she sat down on a swing. He would probably regret this action, but he couldn't help himself. Eli picked up his smiling, babbling daughter in one arm and his son in the other, and walked over to introduce himself.

"My name is Eli Quinn. I have a spare binky in my daughter's bag if you think it'll help."

The mysterious raven-haired woman pretended to cough but he realized she was just covering a sniffle. And when she blinked up those honey-brown eyes at him, his heart took another shot. *Way to go, Quinn.*

And then something seemed to dawn on her as her eyes widened. "Right. Her binky. That's what she wants. Why didn't I think of that?"

She made a beeline for her vehicle. It had to be hers because it was the only other one in the lot. Eli didn't take her walking away personally. He knew exactly what it was like to have a child who wouldn't stop crying and the overwhelming feeling of failure that came with not being able to help.

He walked back to the baby swing and returned Olivia to her happiest place. She giggled as he gently rocked the swing back and forth. Oliver was much happier playing on his own in the sandbox.

A few moments later, the infant quieted and her mother returned.

"I don't know how to thank you. I'm really new at this and this is my first time to be left alone with her for this long." She flashed her eyes at him as she seemed to catch herself. But catch herself at what? Admitting she'd never been alone with her child? "Anyway, I appreciate the reminder. It's exactly what she wanted."

Suddenly he was looking into those honey-golds again. "You'll get the hang of it. It's not easy being a new parent. Don't be so hard on yourself."

"I'm not." Her answer came quickly. Too quickly. That and the fact that she immediately bit down on her bottom lip like she was trying to stop herself from saying more sent up a warning flare. Eli would blame it on the fact that he had a sheriff for a cousin before he'd admit that he wanted to get to know the stranger better. It was probably just his concern for the welfare of a child who couldn't be more than two-months-old that had him needing to dig deeper into her situation.

Not to mention the fact that he'd noticed she didn't volunteer her name.

"What brings you to Gunner?" he asked casually.

"Pit stop. The baby started crying and I realized that I forgot to burp her after her last meal. I figured she had gas pain and I couldn't stand driving while she sounded so sad."

Eli was surprised at the honesty in her admission. He figured sharing a little bit about himself might just help him gain a little bit of her trust. Nothing about her fashionable jeans or caring nature screamed criminal. "The first time I heard my son cry, I panicked."

His admission garnered a half smile followed by a look of disbelief.

"There's no way I believe you." She diverted her gaze and shook her head.

"It's true. I probably shouldn't admit that to anyone and I'm pretty sure I just lost my man card—"

Well, that comment really got her laughing. "I highly doubt it."

Her shoulders relaxed a little bit as she gazed down at the little pink bundle in her arms. "She's not mine. She belongs to my sister. I'm just babysitting for the day and a little out of my league." This time when she smiled at him, warmth spread through him like a ray of sunshine after a long, cold winter day.

"Dangerous," he mumbled.

"Sorry, what was that? I didn't hear you."

He made an excuse and then did the second thing he never thought he would do. He offered the ranch. "My family has a home twenty minutes from here. You're welcome to kill some time there. We pretty much have every baby item known to man."

She stared at him like he was an ax murderer.

"You aren't from around here, are you?" It wasn't uncommon for folks to open up their homes to strangers and especially ones with kids who looked like they needed a hand up. The recent crime rash that had swept through Gunner had made many folks gun shy about offering hospitality. Eli could hold his own.

"I'm from Fort Worth."

His gaze must've narrowed because she immediately asked, "Is there something wrong with Fort Worth?"

3

"Bad memory. That's all."

The look on Eli's face said there was more to the story. Normally, Emery wouldn't be able to resist asking for details. This time, she dropped the subject because she wasn't there to make friends. Besides, if she got him talking about himself, he might think it was okay to ask questions about her. Details about her and her life were off limits.

Eli was tall, six-foot-four-inches if Emery had to guess, with the kind of chiseled jaw that had just enough stubble on it to be considered sexy. Then there were his muscles for days that were easy to see as they strained and stretched against the cotton material of his shirt as he pushed his daughter on the swing.

The man had two children, a boy and a girl. Both about as adorable as they come. And, because she'd checked, no wedding ring. The realization shouldn't bring a shiver of awareness but it did.

"I'm not much for big cities." The hint of disdain in his voice when he said those words had her wondering even more about the story behind them.

She eyed him up and down, telling herself that she was just evaluating a potential threat. His warmth was the kind that couldn't be faked. His kindness had touched her in a place that had been long guarded.

"Thank you for your offer but I'm going to have to turn you down." Emery couldn't afford to be distracted. Figuring out what was going on with her sister, who still hadn't called, was her second priority. The first being taking care of Aria and keeping her safe like Haven had asked. Considering Haven had asked all of three favors in Emery's entire life, and this one being the most important, Emery wanted to do right by her sister.

"I didn't mean...that wasn't intended to scare you."

She cast her gaze down and shuffled her feet a couple of times. "No. It didn't—"

Eli shot her a look that basically called her out on the fact she wasn't being one hundred percent truthful.

"Okay. You got me. That freaked me out a little bit. I'm just passing through and..."

"You don't have to make an excuse for me. This is a small town. Hospitality comes naturally here and most people know my family. I took for granted you don't.

It's really no big deal. I just thought you needed a hand up when it came to the little one. But you have this under control and you're probably smart not to go to a stranger's house."

If only it was true that she had caring for Aria under control. She also needed to be able to make a few calls. She'd memorized a friend's number years ago when she still knew people's phone numbers. Now, she didn't even know her sister's offhand, not that it would probably do any good.

"Thanks for the offer." She felt way too vulnerable already. It was unthinkable to go home with a stranger no matter how handsome or well-known he was in town. Although she'd spent her entire life in bigger cities, she'd heard stories about this kind of hospitality in smaller towns. It was nice. There was a warmth and charm about this place.

"Well. I promised my little guys that I would take them into the bakery across the street for a treat." He paused. "Nice meeting you, Ms...."

"You, too." Those two words rushed out of Emery's mouth in part so she wouldn't be tempted to mention her real name. Keeping Eli Quinn out of the loop was for the best. "Have a great rest of your day." To punctuate her sentence, she turned and walked away toward a nearby jogging trail. It was probably just the stressful morning that she'd been through, but walking away from a strong man capable of having her back in an emergency brought on an unwelcome sense of vulnerability. It was a shame she and Eli hadn't met under normal circumstances. A small part of her that she'd buried a long time ago picked that time to perk up, reminding her that she had a beating heart in her chest and he was the kind of person she'd want to get to know better.

She heard Eli call his son over and she refused to look back for fear that she would have even more regret for letting him walk away. On the one hand, his home could have turned out to be just what she needed, a shelter in the storm. On the other, she could've been putting her and Aria in more danger.

There was nothing about this man that screamed serial killer or that she would be in danger if she took him up on his offer, and it was a shame that her first instinct had to be to protect herself when someone extended hospitality. That was the world she lived in. One that had her locking her doors during the day when she was home and setting an alarm at night. At least until Haven was back.

At least Aria was calm now, sucking happily on her binky. From what Emery could tell of the past six weeks, the little girl went from napping to feeding to being entertained by the slightest things and then repeat.

Haven hadn't once complained about the responsibilities of caring for a newborn on her own. She'd been more than ready to take on the role of mother and Emery wondered if part of the reason for that was the fact that she'd been a second mother to her for most of their life. But the decision to have Aria on her own had been one that Haven hadn't taken lightly. And even though Emery and Haven had always been close, her sister had withheld the pregnancy news until she'd been in her second trimester.

Emery risked a glance toward the parking lot. Eli's truck was parked a safe distance from her car. He must've walked over to the bakery with his kiddos. Her stomach groaned and gargled, reminding her that she hadn't eaten. A caffeine IV would be nice about now.

The trek back to her vehicle was slow. Emery checked her niece's diaper. Satisfied it was still clean and dry, she secured Aria in her special seat. The baby had been fed, changed, and any and all gas was now out of her system. Emery made a mental note to keep track of the binky. It had been a godsend.

Back in the driver seat, Emery paused long enough to pull the cell phone from her pocket. The random thought occurred to her that her sister might've actually loaded her information into the contacts. After a quick check, Emery realized there was no such luck.

She gripped the phone so tight her knuckles went white, thinking how odd it was that she could remember a phone number from five years ago but couldn't recite anyone's current number other than her own.

This time, the engine choked and then died when she turned the key over.

ELI HAD BARELY GOTTEN the kids settled in their high chairs and their favorite treats in front of them when he looked up to find the mysterious park dweller standing just inside the door and staring directly at him. He waved her over and got to his feet.

"My car won't start. I don't have a whole lot of cash on me and I just changed cell phones and forgot my old one." The thought crossed his mind that she seemed guilty of something. He would never put his children in danger by helping a criminal, but then he remembered how upset she'd been at the park when she couldn't seem to soothe her niece. Scenarios popped into his mind, and the one that seemed most plausible was that she was helping her sister withhold the child due to a custody battle.

"I'm no mechanic but I'm happy to take a look if you'd like me to." His offer was met with a nervous nod of approval.

"Only if it wouldn't be too much trouble." She shifted her weight from her left foot to her right as she looked down at the baby in her arms. "She's still so little and I need a place to take care of her while I figure out what's going on with my car."

The mystery woman's stomach growled.

"Done. I can make sure your car gets fixed. I'll take a look at it myself and if I can't fix it I know somebody who can." She looked like she was about to mount a protest. "I'm owed a few favors, so no one will ask questions and there won't be any charges."

"I'm really sorry to ask so much of you when we just met." Again, she shifted her weight from one foot to the other. "This is really awkward of me and I—"

Eli held up a hand to stop her from continuing. "It's really not that big of a deal. Folks around here look after each other. Speaking of which, when was the last time you ate?"

A red blush crawled up her cheeks. Oh hell, he hadn't meant to embarrass her.

"My sister-in-law is part owner of this place. The food here is amazing. I'll get a menu for you."

Her top teeth scraped across her bottom lip and he could tell that she was considering his offer.

"I do have a little bit of cash on me. It does smell amazing in here." She seemed to be calculating what she could afford to spend.

"Your money is no good here. Let me get this. It's the least I can do."

She tilted her head to one side as she examined him. His heart shouldn't beat so fast against his rib cage under her assessment. It'd been a long time ago since Eli was a blushing teenager. And yet on some level that was exactly how he felt with the stranger.

"What's in it for you? I mean, that came out wrong. Why are you being so nice?" Her head stayed cocked to one side. It saddened him that someone had so much trouble accepting kindness from a stranger. It was the most normal thing in the world for him to offer to help.

"The satisfaction of helping someone who needs it." He shrugged. "I blame it on the way I was brought up. Ranchers have always had to depend on each other. So, it's second nature."

"Well, this is too much. I can't let you do that." Her jaw set with determination.

Well, that really made Eli chuckle. Hospitality, a sense of community and family, those were the reasons he'd stuck around Gunner instead of moving away like most of his brothers had. Besides, he couldn't imagine living on a better ranch than Quinnland and cattle ranching was in his blood.

"I'd hate to shock you or diminish this great act of kindness you think I am presently engaged in, but this is just how folks do things here. I already told you. Someone needs a hand up, we offer it. If it hadn't been me in the park, it would've been any one of these nice folks in my place." Was it wrong that he was more than grateful that it had been him? Probably. Or maybe just stupid. Either way, he was relieved he'd had the honor.

"I have to take your word for it. Thank you. Your hospitality is above and beyond anything I could've expected."

"Good. Like I said, a dear family friend by the name of Becky Stillwater owns this place and her niece, Savannah, is the sister-in-law I mentioned. Neither of them would let you starve. We take care of visitors in this town but it's nothing like how we take care of our own. Now, what can I get you from the counter?"

A hesitant smile flashed across her face. He'd take it. "Do I smell fresh croissants? And coffee? I haven't had any caffeine today."

"Don't say another word." Her admission got Eli's feet moving. He couldn't function without coffee if he tried and was thankful that he hadn't had to in recent memory. He collected her order and placed it on a tray. By the time he got back, he was happy to see that the mystery woman had settled into a chair. Granted, it was pushed back a little far from the table and he couldn't help but notice that she positioned it so that she could see that exit.

Ready for a quick escape? He already knew she wasn't a bill runner. There'd be no point. He'd already paid for her breakfast.

He set the offerings on the round table. "Would you like me to hold your niece while you eat breakfast?"

The look she shot him could make the blood in his veins turn to ice. She quickly recovered as her gaze darted from Oliver to Olivia, both of whom were happily playing and babbling to each other.

Her hands looked like a crane couldn't forcibly remove them from her niece as she studied him. She tried to balance the baby and pick up the croissant. She lifted her knee to take some of the baby's weight.

Shoulders deflated, she said, "I guess it would be okay if you wanted to hold her if it's not too much trouble."

"In case you haven't noticed the two little ones with me, I have experience with rugrats. I'll just sit down, so you can hand her to me. Once you eat breakfast, I'll hand her back and then start making some calls."

Leary brown eyes stared at him. They bounced from Oliver to Olivia and back. She seemed to realize how difficult it would be to manage holding an infant while trying to eat breakfast and drink coffee.

Reluctantly, she leaned toward him and handed over the little pink bundle. Eli noticed a subtle shift in the position of her chair that put her between him and the exit.

"How old did you say she is?" He figured it was a safe question. Getting her talking might help her shoulders relax a little.

"Six weeks." She took a sip of coffee and then

locked gazes with him. After a mewl sound, she said, "The coffee is amazing. I mean, like, really amazing."

"Becky Stillwater has owned this place for decades. By now, she has pretty much everything perfected." He laughed. It was the reason he came into town every Sunday with his kiddos.

As if to test his theory, she picked up the croissant and took a bite. A satisfied smile brought up the corners of her heart-shaped pink lips. "Mmm. How is this as good as the coffee?"

"Secret recipe, I guess. I'll tell Ms. Stillwater that she has another satisfied customer." Eli chuckled again. His mystery breakfast companion took down the croissant like she was eating at a hot dog eating contest on the Fourth of July. He didn't mind helping her. He was being truthful about that. He had a feeling that he could do a whole lot more for her if he knew what her real troubles were.

She glanced at him from behind the rim of the coffee mug.

"My name is Emery. And you're holding Aria."

4

Emery hoped she didn't end up regretting giving her name to Eli. She purposely left off her last name, hoping to shield him from as much of the truth as she could. But here was the thing. She needed help. There was no way she could figure out a way to fix her car without using a credit card or leaving a trail, figure out what was going on with her sister, *and* take care of Aria.

The first priority was Aria's safety. Emery had a sinking feeling in the pit of her stomach as the morning started to disappear that this ordeal might last longer than a few hours as she'd hoped. That meant she needed to find a place to stay for the day and possibly overnight. She wasn't kidding when she told Eli that she only had a little cash, and something told her she needed to hang on to as much of it as possible.

This was the first time the notion that this situation could really drag on struck her. And it hit her like a bucket of bricks. She needed food and shelter, a safe place to care for the baby while she did a little digging around into her sister's life.

There was an inn next door to the bakery. But after Haven's warning to hide, using a credit card seemed like a risky move. It was best to be overly cautious after what had happened this morning with the blacked-out truck.

A tall man who looked to be in his early-to-mid sixties wearing a cowboy hat and jeans walked over to the table. His skin was weather-worn, and she noticed that he walked with a slight limp. She tucked her chin to her chest, trying to shield herself from view. The last thing she needed was to leave a trail of witnesses. It was so foreign to have to think like that, like witnesses and trucks with blacked-out windows practically running her off the road were as normal as waking up in the morning. Speaking of which, this morning's run-in felt like a lifetime ago and yet only a few short hours had passed. Looking back, she was a little surprised at her ability to adapt in such a stressful situation.

In Austin, there would be help, but no one with room or the kind environment that would be conducive to a baby. Going there seemed like a bad move. It had been a knee-jerk reaction to the panic she'd felt.

"Fancy seeing you here," the older gentleman said to Eli.

Out of the corner of her eye, she saw him pat Eli on the shoulder. They exchanged smiles and she could tell that they were more than casual acquaintances.

"You know I usually bring the kiddos into town on Sunday mornings." The fact that Eli had squared off with the older man, like he was being protective of her, warmed her heart. She also noticed and appreciated that he made no attempt to introduce her.

The older man's gaze bounced from her and then back to Eli. An uncomfortable silence sat between them. Fortunately, he didn't seem to dwell on it. Better yet, he didn't ask questions. "I'm heading back to the ranch, I can take the little guys home with me."

"I'd appreciate that, Dakota. I'll let Marianne know they're on their way. Oliver will be ready to work out some of the sugar he just had before they both drop like flies." Eli's warm smile reached his eyes when he talked about his children. He turned his attention toward Emery and a dozen butterflies released in her stomach. "Will you be okay to take her back while I get Oliver and Olivia settled in Dakota's truck?"

She nodded and took Aria from him. Her hands grazed his in the exchange and electricity pinged from contact.

Emery couldn't remember the last time a man had had that kind of effect on her. She chalked the rush of feelings up to overwrought emotions. It had been a day. And a glance at the clock on the wall said the day was just getting started.

Eli and his friend, Dakota, took Oliver and Olivia outside. Her newfound friend couldn't take more than a couple of steps without somebody waving, shaking his hand or trying to get his attention even just to return a smile. He wasn't kidding about this town being friendly and him being well-known.

The thought was comforting. Eli returned a few minutes later. It was almost strange to see him without a kid in his arms. As he walked toward her from across the room, she took note of all the eyes on him, following him, looking like they'd be thrilled if he acknowledged their presence. When she really thought about it, it was a lot like being with her ex once his songs had started hitting the charts.

"Sorry about that. Dakota is the foreman at my family's ranch. He's known my father since long before I was born." Eli reclaimed his seat and she didn't immediately speak. She did, however, take note of just how influential he seemed to be in his community.

Emery couldn't say that she knew a whole lot about life on a ranch, but one big enough to have a foreman was probably doing okay. And based on everyone's reaction to Eli, his family had either been around for generations or were the wealthiest people in town.

The man sitting across from her was so down-to-earth and real. Could he be rich? Based on the rough feel of his hands, he had enough calluses to say that he was used to hard work. "Can I ask a question?"

He nodded.

"How many people live at your home?"

"On the ranch? Well, let's see, at the main house I've lost count. My father owns it and the place is called Casa Grande."

Emery was rusty on her high school Spanish. However, the name of his family's house in Spanish was literally *big house*. And she took note of the fact that he'd said the main house. How many others were there?

He continued, "As far as people go, my father is out of town, so he's not around. Marianne, our housekeeper and the woman who was basically a surrogate mother to me and my six brothers, lives there and she helps out a lot with my kiddos and the other new family members." He chuckled, and his deep timbre reverberated through her, stirring up all kinds of tingly sensations in her stomach.

She ignored them.

"My family's been growing by leaps and bounds. All of my brothers are married or in the process of getting married, so I can't keep up anymore with the numbers. Suffice to say, at any given moment the house is bustling with activity. Oh, and Marianne is probably the best cook in Texas. She makes three square meals a day, despite all of us being old enough to take care of ourselves. Why do you ask?"

"I was thinking that while my car is being looked at that I might need a better place for Aria. Taking care of her out of the back seat of my car today has been challenging at best. At worst, it's made me want to cry. And I don't cry."

"Well then, how about we head back to the main house while I make a call to have your car towed to Big Ben's shop? You and Aria will be a lot more comfortable there than anywhere else." Eli stood up and she noticed once again just how tall of a man he was. Her stomach did more of that freefall action. So, she ignored it and followed his lead. He caught her last-ditch desperate glance toward her empty coffee cup. She wasn't kidding before. That was seriously the best coffee she'd ever had in her life.

"They'll fix you a to-go cup."

She started to tell him not to go to the trouble but it was too late. With a satisfied smirk, he was already heading toward the counter. He ordered two cups and the three of them walked out the door a few moments later.

"I can have a quick look at your car while you buckle your niece in my truck." He balanced the coffee cups on his arm and took the keys she'd fished out of her pocket. Skillfully, he managed to get his own set of keys out and click the key fob to unlock the doors.

He managed to open the door to his truck and put the coffees in cup holders in the front seat. She noted that he was skilled with his hands before giving herself a mental slap; that was the last thing she should be noticing at the moment. He retrieved Aria's car seat out of the back of Emery's hatchback and relocated it to the back seat of his vehicle, placing it in the middle of his children's car seats. Dakota had spare car seats in his vehicle, which made transferring the kids around much easier. Watching the ease and confidence with which he moved, not to mention how quickly he managed to secure the seat, she realized he was on a whole different level with this childcare thing. It also occurred to her that she needed to grab her weekend bag and Aria's diaper bag.

Emery decided taking him up on his offer was maybe the smartest thing she'd done so far today. She and Aria would be secluded on a ranch and yet there would be enough people around to make her feel like she hadn't just agreed to go home with a serial killer.

With Aria secured, Emery climbed into the passenger seat and exhaled. She picked up the coffee and took a sip. It really was heaven on earth. She watched as her newfound friend popped the hood of her car and examined underneath.

He checked a few things, nothing she could name. She knew zero about what made cars run. She got her oil changed on time, made sure there was gas in the tank, but that was the extent of her knowledge. Her June Bug, named for its shape and the fact that it was red, had gotten her through some interesting years. She'd packed what little belongings she'd had in it and moved home to Fort Worth when her time in Austin had come to a close.

She caught herself checking out Eli's strong, muscled, broad back. And she was mortified when he glanced in her direction and caught her.

Emery jerked her head in the opposite direction. *Smooth move, Em.* To make matters worse, she acted like she was studying the coffee cup in the console. And then in the next few seconds her hood was closed, and Eli was walking toward her. The smirk on his face told her everything she needed to know about how sly she'd been.

"Your problem is out of my league."

Eli reclaimed the driver's seat and picked up his cup of coffee. The red blush crawling up Emery's cheeks made her even more attractive. Not that she needed any help in that department or he needed to keep paying attention. *Off limits*, he reminded himself.

"Excuse me." Her voice came out as a croak and that was another reason to smile. He wasn't the only one off his game. Not that he was trying to 'game' her. It had just been a really long time since he was this amused or thought a reaction like hers was this appealing.

"Your car. I couldn't see anything wrong with it and now that service is going by way of computer chips and technology it'll most likely have to be hooked up to a diagnostic machine to figure out why the ignition won't turn over." He made a quick phone call to the garage. "I left the keys under the floormat for the mechanic."

"Oh. Sorry." More of that embarrassment flamed her beautiful cheeks.

His chest squeezed, and he did his level best to ignore it. Even if the woman in his passenger seat was the prettiest he'd seen in longer than he cared to remember, she was from Fort Worth. There were a whole lot of other obvious reasons it was a bad idea to think about Emery more than in just the light of trying to help her for a day.

His passenger was in some kind of trouble. He believed that she was telling him the truth about Aria being her niece and that her sister had asked her to keep the baby for the day. It was what she wasn't telling him that sent his radar flaring.

If he had to venture a guess, he'd say the trouble

she was in had something to do with her sister. Maybe he could get her talking about her family and find out a little bit more. It was possible he could offer a lot more assistance than a roof over her head and help with fixing her vehicle.

"Is it just you and your sister in your family?" He navigated onto the road and toward home.

"Yes. I didn't know my father. He left not long after I was born. My mother brought my sister and me up on her own. She died a few years ago."

"I'm sorry for your loss." He of all people knew the pain of losing a mother.

"Thank you. She was a remarkable person, my mother." She took a sip of her coffee. "I still miss her."

"I bet you do."

Emery got quiet and he regretted bringing up a subject that seemed to cause her pain. And then she quickly turned the tables. "I thought you said you lived with your father, but you said he's not home. Is your mother around?"

"My father is in Dallas. He'll be home any day now. As for my mother, well, she's been gone most of my life." He couldn't help but feel for Oliver and Olivia. They, too, would grow up never knowing what it was like to have a mother. "She passed away when my youngest brother was born."

"I'm really sorry to hear that, Eli."

A moment of respectful silence passed before either seemed to feel the need to talk again.

"I appreciate your kindness, but it's been so long I barely remember her anymore. Doesn't change how I feel about her, though. My father, on the other hand, is his own force of nature. He built a successful cattle ranch from nothing and continues to run it to this day."

"He sounds like an amazing person."

"He's something all right. He was much better at cattle ranching than he was at bringing up seven rowdy boys—"

"Hold on a minute. I wasn't certain that I'd heard you correctly before. But you did say there were seven children in your family, all boys?"

"That's correct."

"I cannot even imagine that." There was a wistful quality to her voice.

"Not the family type?"

"It's not that. I just can't imagine having *that* many children to look after. Aria is a handful and she's tiny." The wistfulness turned to amazement.

Eli laughed. "I can blow your mind even more than that."

"Well this ought to be good." He liked that she was starting to relax a little bit more around him. He couldn't exactly pinpoint why that seemed so important to him. It just did.

"I have five cousins. All males. They spent most of their childhood running around the ranch with us. Oh, and two of my brothers are twins."

"Consider my mind blown. Hold on a second." She started counting on her fingers and he knew what was coming next before she said it. "That's twelve men. Do they all look like you?"

"What do you mean?"

She turned her face in the opposite direction when she said, "I don't know. Tall, muscles, good-looking?"

Well, now Eli really laughed. "I don't know if I would consider any of the guys good-looking, let alone myself. But we're all built similarly and around the same height."

A mix between a laugh and a chortle burst from her mouth. "You must not have any mirrors in your house." Those words came out under her breath.

"If that was a compliment, I'll take it." Eli chocked his out of place attraction up to going too long without asking anyone on a date. Yes, he was busy between kiddos and his work at the ranch. But there was more to it than that. In moments of pure honesty, he was still kicking himself for falling for the wrong woman because of the suffering it would cost his children.

5

"You, your brothers and your cousins look similar and there's twelve of you? Have you guys ever thought about making a calendar?"

The reaction Emery got from Eli was priceless. The look on his face was priceless. The grunt that he made...priceless.

"I may have heard that one a time or two growing up." There was no humor in his voice now and yet she couldn't help but think he appreciated the compliment. Especially when he quirked a smile.

His demeanor shifted and he got a lot more serious on a patch of the two-lane highway that she could only imagine led to his family's ranch. "Everything okay?"

"Bad memory. My brother's fiancée was in a crash along this stretch of road recently. Every time I drive past here, I'm reminded that bad things can happen to good people and at just how quickly life can turn on a dime." He quickly added, "Her situation worked out fine. She came out of the wreck with just a few injuries. Nothing that won't heal."

"That's good news, right?" She wasn't exactly sure why she added the last word, except that there seemed to be more to the story.

"It is. Better yet, she and my brother seem to have found real happiness together. The two had been best friends in high school. We all used to joke they should just go ahead and date way back when. They'd been inseparable, and we had to cover for Aiden plenty of times because he couldn't tear himself away from her. It's good to see them together and happy. The thought of how things could have turned out is not so great."

"It seems like they're lucky to have found each other again."

He nodded.

Emery waited for more questions to come about her situation. His comment from a few moments ago hadn't gone unnoticed or unheard, and she figured it was for her benefit. Bad things *did* happen to good people. He'd been clear with his message. She could agree there. In her case, she had no idea what she was up against.

"Mind if I ask a personal question?" His question broke through the quiet.

Emery's shoulder muscles tensed. "No. Go right ahead." She wasn't exactly promising an answer, but he could ask. He deserved that much after all the kindness he'd shown her and Aria so far.

"Does Aria have a father in the picture? Is that why you had to take her and get out of town?" She hesitated, and he quickly added, "You don't have to tell me anything you don't want to. I'm just trying to assess what I might be up against. If there's an abusive ex in the picture for your sister, I should know about it in case he shows up at Quinnland."

That was the moment that she realized that she might be about to walk into what sounded like cattlemen royalty. His family had a ranch named after them? When she really thought about it, it made sense. She remembered Eli mentioning that his father had built a successful business from the ground up.

"My sister is a single parent." She immediately realized that didn't exactly cover the territory he was talking about. Being a single parent could mean that her sister was divorced or that there was a baby daddy somewhere in the background. "Correction, my sister became a mother through in vitro fertilization. She went to a fertility clinic. There's no father in the picture to speak of."

Eli nodded his head. "Makes sense. I'll cancel out any possibility of an issue with custody."

"Right. No one will be coming to claim rights over

Aria. My sister decided to do this on her own. She turned thirty last year and decided to move forward with her plans to start a family." Emery hoped she wasn't over sharing but the man was putting himself in danger by helping her whether he knew it or not. The thought Emery could be putting his sweet little angels in harm's way along with him struck like a physical blow. She thought about her options and realized how few she had. No one seemed to have followed her to Gunner, Texas. The coast was clear. She could hide out for a day and then go find her sister once night fell.

Eli did bring up a good point about a possible father being in the background somewhere. That couldn't be right, though. Could it?

Haven could have lied about going to the clinic...

No. Her sister didn't have a deceitful bone in her body. She especially wouldn't lie to Emery. They'd always been honest with each other. Even when Emery was going through her wild child phase, she'd confided in Haven. Her sister had listened intently to all the stories of what it was like to be on the road with a musician.

There were plenty of stories to tell of parties and the late-night eating. Being on the road had been fun for the first year, maybe two. By the third year, Emery was beginning to feel like she had no home. As the fourth had winded down, she knew she was out of her element.

To make matters worse, the more success her boyfriend had, the more aggressive other women in pursuit of him became. In truth, in that fourth-year, she felt like she had too much competition for his attention. And yet, she stuck around for the fifth before finally being able to let go. It was a good learning experience, though. Chet had thrived on the attention and she was fairly certain he left the groupies at the door. Although, to be honest, one of his bandmate's wives gave Emery the impression that might not be so true.

Since Eli was going way above and beyond the call to offer help, he deserved to know a little bit about the situation. Plus, it might be nice to have someone to help think through what could possibly be going on.

"My sister asked me to watch Aria. The truth is, I have no idea what's going on. Haven, that's her name, showed up before the sun came up this morning and left the baby in my care. She'd been saying that she was going to do just that, so in my half-asleep state it didn't strike me as odd as it probably should have."

"Was that the first time she'd left you alone with her daughter?"

"Not exactly, but she'd never left Aria at my apartment and then taken off before and never longer than an hour or two." Emery debated telling him about the truck.

"Thank you for trusting me, Emery." Those words spurred her to share a little more.

"You should know that my sister might be in danger. She took my phone and replaced it with this one that I'm keeping in my pocket. I can't for the life of me figure out why she would do that. She's always been law-abiding." Finding answers and fast while she still had a possibility to help her sister overruled the need to keep secrets. Emery had always been a private person, so talking about her and her family was foreign ground.

"I'd like to help." There was so much sincerity in those words.

"Putting you and your family in danger isn't fair. I probably said too much already. Once we get my car fixed, I'd like to get back on the road." She had no idea where she would go or what that meant but she didn't want to overstay her welcome. "I can figure this out on my own. Besides, my sister will probably call at any minute and all of this will be cleared up." She couldn't contain the hope in her voice that those words could be true. The sense of dread settling in the pit of her stomach seemed to know otherwise.

"I understand your position and I respect your wishes. In the meantime, I make a pretty good sounding board. Our family is no stranger to crime. We've been through a lot and have come out stronger for it. We are private people but our position in the community makes it a little rough to stay under the radar."

Emery gasped. She brought her hand to her mouth. "Oh. Right. I hadn't thought about how much visibility your family gets. I only focused on how remote your ranch seemed."

"No one gets on the property or past security without permission. Dakota is in our employment, even though he's more like one of the family. We have a few full-time ranch hands who rarely ever have the need to come into the main house. There's a bunkhouse attached to the barn and that's where they spend their time when they're not out doing work, which is pretty much from early in the morning until supper. These men aren't the type to get in anyone's business, and they are not a chatty bunch. Other than that, we have Marianne in the main house. She's been with us a long time. There won't be a problem with her giving you away. That being said, if I've lost track of how many people we have in the main house, so would everyone else. I doubt anyone would pay attention to a new face."

"It sounds like we might be able to blend into the woodwork." The second hint that she was about to spend time with one of the wealthiest families in Texas came when Eli turned into a drive.

A security guard at the gate waved before the mechanical gate opened. They passed with a wave. Winding down the drive, the house came into view. Casa Grande was too modest a description of the massive home that came into view. For starters, she'd never visited a home that had its own parking lot.

She liked the idea of security and the sound of blending in. The place sounded almost too good to be true.

6

"You didn't tell me the place was like *this*."

Eli parked his truck and turned to his passenger, ignoring the shot to the center of his chest that came with looking at her. "You didn't ask."

"Smart-aleck," she teased under her breath.

"Did you just call me a name?" Despite the heavy conversation, he appreciated the break in tension.

"Me? Nah." She smiled at him and even though the smile didn't reach her honey-brown eyes it still made her even more beautiful. "Still, you could have prepared me a little better for this."

"My bad. When you grow up in a place, I guess you forget how it might look to others."

"I can't even imagine what life must've been like here."

"Not everything is as it seems on the surface." His tone was sharper than he wanted it to be. Without diving into an explanation, he exited the truck. By the time he made it around to the passenger side, Emery had already climbed in the back seat and was pulling out the baby carrier.

Carrier in arm and bags on every shoulder, she stopped and searched his eyes. He could almost feel her peeling back the layers to look deeper.

"Ready?"

She nodded, slowly. Apologetically? "I imagine everyone has a story to tell. Don't they?"

"No matter what something looks like on the surface, nothing is perfect." Eli walked side-by-side to the front door. It was unlocked, as always, so he opened it. Emery took two steps inside and froze.

"Wow. Just wow." She stood in the foyer, seeming to take in the grandness of it all. "Color me impressed."

"It's just a house, like any other. Made of brick and mortar." When she didn't argue, he said, "I need to check on my kiddos. Think you'll be okay in the kitchen?"

"Point me in a direction. Any chance you have a laptop in there I could use?"

"Probably not, but I'd be happy to locate mine and bring it to you. Kitchen is straight back. I texted Marianne when I was looking at your car to let her know we were coming. No one will be surprised to have you here." He pointed directly down the hall.

"Sounds like a plan. Thank you, again, for everything you're doing for me and Aria. I don't think I've adequately expressed how grateful I am that I met you at the park today."

Those words shouldn't send electrical impulses racing through Eli's body. It was a simple thank you. *Way to keep it toned down, Quinn.*

He had a feeling if he'd met her at another time, or another place she was exactly the kind of person he would want to get to know better.

"Make yourself at home. Coffee is not as good as at Becky Stillwater's place, but it's close and it gets the job done."

She nodded and headed toward the kitchen. He liked that she felt comfortable enough in his family home to be on her own.

After checking on Oliver and Olivia, only to find them napping in their room, he located his laptop and made his way into the kitchen. The babies all seemed to be on the same sleep schedule today because Aria had dozed off as well. All Eli could remember from when his kiddos were around that age was how much they ate, messed in their diapers, and slept. It felt like someone hit the reset button every few hours when they did it all again.

"Looks like somebody's conked out." He remembered Oliver and Olivia doing the same thing after crying themselves to sleep when Camille left. At least with Oliver, his ex-wife had been around a little while. Eli had kept up his normal schedule working the ranch. Olivia was a different story altogether. Camille left them almost immediately and he'd done everything on his own with Marianne's help after. Two little kids with one dad. Yes, he'd felt outnumbered.

"Yeah, thankfully." Emery had a fresh cup of coffee sitting on the table in front of her and a cell phone that she'd been staring at when he walked in. Even though she admitted to only having her niece a couple of hours and under stressful conditions, he couldn't help but notice how tired and concerned she looked when she gazed down at Aria.

"My kids' mother walked out not long after Olivia was born and—"

The shocked and disgusted look Emery shot stopped him before he could end his sentence. "How could any person walk away from something so tiny, so weak, and so innocent?"

He didn't have a good answer for that one considering he felt the same way.

"I can tell you what she said when she left." Suddenly, the rim of his coffee cup got real interesting. "This whole family 'thing' isn't right for me. I made a mistake."

Emery grunted her disapproval.

"She went on to explain that having children and a husband didn't turn out to be as fun as she expected it to be." He paused there because he could scarcely believe the words even though he'd heard them firsthand.

"No offense, but your ex sounds like a real piece of work."

"I was the one who made a mistake. I should never have believed that she could change her life so drastically for me or anyone else. That's on me." And he never intended to make that same mistake again.

"People can be real jerks, you know?"

That was the understatement of the century. He nodded before bringing his gaze up to meet hers, realizing she wasn't talking about only his ex anymore. It was a blanket statement that covered all the insincere people walking around in the world.

"It's my fault, not hers. But I couldn't agree more with your statement."

"How so? How could her walking out on one of the most beautiful little girls in the world end up being your fault? Were you mean to her? I mean, you don't seem like the type, but you can never really know..."

"No." He had to chuckle at that. He opened the laptop and logged in. "I treated her like a princess."

"So, you were nothing but nice to her."

"That's right." Looking back, he'd put her too much

on a pedestal instead of making her his partner in life. She'd wanted to be taken care of and he'd obliged, figuring they would grow old together and the differences he'd noticed in their personalities would eventually work themselves out.

"And she fell in love with you?"

"I thought so." After she left, he realized there was no way she could've truly loved him and the kids and still walked out of their lives. She was all excitement and a love-you-in-the-moment person. Like a star that burns itself out from burning too bright. She'd gone all-in and then fizzled.

She'd been honest with him when she'd told him that she didn't want to fake a relationship for anyone's sake. And as awful as it had been, that honesty had been the one thing that had made everything bearable; he didn't want Oliver and Olivia to realize that their mother didn't want to be there, and if he'd learned anything from his own childhood, it was that children were very perceptive about that sort of thing.

"And you loved her right back. Harder than you've ever fallen for anyone else."

"Hard and fast." Looking back, he'd fallen for his ex too fast. Next time, if he let himself go down that path again, he'd take his time and make certain that he could trust what he felt. He'd make even more certain the other person reciprocated. "I can't help but think there was something missing and that's the reason she left. What that missing 'thing' was is anyone's guess. We didn't talk about things the way we probably should have. I had eyes. It was as plain as the nose on my face that she wasn't happy."

"Love seems to come with blinders."

Eli wouldn't argue Emery's point. To say he'd been blindsided was a lot like saying cows spent most of their time in pastures. "There were signs. I just chose to ignore them."

"Like what?" She tilted her head to one side.

"She basically cut herself off from her parents. She stopped communicating with them over a disagreement. Told me that she hadn't spoken to either one of them in four years." It had raised a red flag that he'd initially ignored, figuring her parents might be like T.J. Several of Eli's brothers couldn't wait to get off the ranch after graduation. In T.J.'s case, it was warranted.

"Did she tell you what the disagreement was about?"

"Not at first. Eventually, I got it out of her but she was already pregnant with Oliver. She said they didn't like how she was handling her trust fund. She said they kept getting on her for spending money on lavish vacations. So, she just stopped returning their calls." A year after that, they cut her off financially and that was around the time the two of them had met. He suspected part of the reason she fell in love with him so hard and so fast was because she was about to run out of money. It was a harsh reality that he hadn't wanted to consider before.

"I can't even imagine doing that on purpose. My own dad took off when I was little. If he'd been in my life, I certainly wouldn't cut him off over a financial disagreement."

"I'm sorry that happened to you. I don't understand any man or woman who can walk away from family. Your father missed out on an amazing person when he turned his back on you." It was obvious how devoted Emery was to her sister and niece.

"Thank you." Those two words spoken with such affection packed an emotional punch. "What happened with your wife?"

"After Olivia was born, things got worse between us. My biggest mistake was that I didn't get her talking about it. Marianne asked me if I knew anything about postpartum depression. I guess everyone around us could tell something was off. I searched up the word on the Internet. Somehow, it didn't seem to fit; there's a difference between being depressed and just outright being unhappy, but I figured out the later just a little bit too late. Believe me, I wanted it to be a medical issue. That could be fixed with patience, understanding, and medical help. *That* would go away in time."

"Her unhappiness might not have had anything to do with you."

Eli didn't see how that was possible. He shrugged. "I did my best to make her happy at the time. Hindsight says it wasn't enough. It did make me realize how important communication is in a relationship and how dangerous it is to assume a rough patch will smooth itself out."

She pursed her lips together and nodded like she fully understood. "What about the kids? Do they see her?"

"Camille signed over her parental rights. Said she wouldn't know what to do with the kids if they came to stay with her even for a weekend. She thought it might be too hard on them to go back and forth and said she thought I could provide a more stable life for them. If she had no plans to be in their life permanently it was the best thing she could've done. If she couldn't be bothered to stick around, at least she no intention of constantly disrupting their lives." This was the most Eli had opened up and talked about his ex. Period. A few of the heavy boulders that felt parked on his shoulders seemed to lift. He told himself that it was just easier to talk to a stranger. But that wasn't completely true. Emery's easy nature made it easy to talk to her and he found himself wanting to open up to her and find out what made her tick.

Dredging up his past brought up a surprising

amount of pain. He thought he'd dealt with it and moved on. Guess he bottled it up instead. This should make him feel exposed. There was something different about Emery that caused him to feel like a small piece of the burden he carried on his shoulders was breaking up.

"The past is the past. Time to move on. Besides, talking about my situation won't get us any closer to figuring out what's going on with your sister." Eli didn't want to cross any boundaries, but he wanted to get to know Emery a little better.

Much to his surprise, she brought her hand over to his. Her touch was soft, her skin creamy and smooth.

"You and those beautiful babies deserve so much more. I hope you don't beat yourself up too much over falling for someone who was unable to give herself in return. For what it's worth, it sounds like she was scared or the kind of person who could be charming at first before showing their true colors later. I know one thing is certain. She lost out on what could've been three of the greatest gifts in her life."

Those words struck a chord, soothing the broken parts in him more than he knew better to allow. "I appreciate your kindness." He needed to change the subject and get back on track. He took a sip from his coffee mug, cleared his throat, and then redirected the conversation, taking her hand in his and letting his thumb roll circles in the palm of her hand.

"When it comes to your sister's case, if a child is in danger or there's a threat to a woman and child then ninety-nine percent of the time it comes from the child's father or someone the mother was in a relationship with who saw the baby as a threat."

"Which really doesn't work in this case, considering she had in vitro. What other ideas do you have?"

"Good question. I'm guessing your sister wasn't dating anyone." Emery was already shaking her head before he finished the sentence.

"She would've told me if she had been. And she hasn't dated much since she was left at the altar two years ago."

"Okay." He tapped his finger on the wooden table. "What does she do for a living?"

"She's a paralegal. This is her eighth year at the firm. She works at Rory, Vanderburg, and Scott. She really likes the attorneys that she works with and they seem to like her. She's always being given awards for her dedication, her service or for a case she worked on."

"Has she mentioned dealing with anything high-profile?" Since Eli's cousin was the sheriff and his uncle had held the job before him, he'd heard plenty of stories over the years of criminals threatening to harm them or their families. He figured the same was true at a law firm.

"My sister never talks about work except in a

general sense. She's always seemed content to leave it at the door. She was always far more interested in what I was doing until I started nursing school and then I was working, studying or too tired to spend much time together. Each day started looking like the next."

"Do you love it?"

The question seemed to catch her off guard. Her eyebrow shot up and she pursed her lips together. "I wanted to. My mother worked at a hospital and I think it made me feel closer to her to follow in her footsteps. I love the idea of caring for people more than the reality of it. Mostly, I'm too tired to think about whether I'm happy or not."

"Do you think about leaving nursing school?"

This time, she laughed. "Every day."

"It's none of my business, Emery. But if I've learned one thing it's that life is short and can change on a dime. It's important to do something that makes you eager to jump out of bed every morning."

"Is that the way it is for you on the ranch?" She tilted her head.

"Yes. A bad day on the ranch is better than a great day doing anything else."

"Wow. That gives me a lot to think about. My mindset has been that work is what you do for a living. Finding something stable seemed really important after being on the road so much. But, you make a good point about loving your work." She squeezed his hand.

Since contact made his heart thunder, he decided to circle the conversation back to her sister. "Did your sister love her work?"

"I think so. There was just a lot of it and I know she didn't think that would be a good fit after the baby came."

"What type of law does her firm practice?"

"Mainly corporate stuff. Mergers. Takeovers. That kind of thing. My sister worked long hours and was planning to find something more suitable to motherhood after she was due back from maternity leave. She planned to give them another year at most. The main reason she was holding off is because she liked her job so much."

"Did she say what kind of work she was interested in doing next?" Eli was grasping at straws when it came to the working angle. If she'd been an attorney and especially a defense attorney, he might put more merit into her disappearance being related to her career. Then again, as a paralegal she would have access to sensitive information and that could rankle internal employees if there was a cover-up.

He was most likely grasping at straws when it came to work. Still, the law enforcement officers in his family would tell him to track down every possible angle. He had to start somewhere. Considering work seemed to be Haven's life, it seemed as good a place as any to begin.

"Teaching, for one. She'd made a list of possibilities and put it on her fridge. That's part of what the next six months were supposed to be about. She wanted to give careful consideration to her next move. The firm gave her three months of maternity leave and she'd burned through half of that already. Making a decision without thinking through all the possibilities wasn't her style."

He made a mental note to circle back and reach out to co-workers if this thing continued down the path it was currently on. Technically, no one was missing yet. Haven had asked her sister to babysit. Granted, taking her phone and replacing it with a temporary one was suspicious and extreme. It didn't mean anything bad had happened to her sister. His knowledge of law enforcement made him realize that even an officer would look at the evidence suspiciously. But no crime had been committed yet as far as anyone knew. Sure, the situation was suspect but what kind of report could actually be filed to prevent a crime they weren't certain was happening or had happened?

Speaking of which, it might not hurt to get a professional opinion on the situation. "Have you thought about going to law enforcement?"

"No. I can't. She specifically asked me not to."

Eli took in a deep breath and blew it out slowly. The request complicated matters. "Did she say why?"

Emery shook her head. "She left a note asking for a

little time to sort 'something' out after telling me to hide until she reached out to me with this throwaway phone."

"Have you considered the possibility that it might hurt her more if you didn't go to the police?" The question had to be asked.

"Of course, I have. You think I want to be in this position? I don't want to go against what she asked, and I don't want anything bad to happen to her. I think the main thing she was concerned about was Aria's safety and that's why she left her with me. I'm walking in a field of nails with a blindfold on here."

Again, his mind snapped to this having something to do with the child. "We need to rewind. How did your sister decide which clinic to go to?"

"That's a great question. Normally, we share all the important events in our lives. But I didn't know about Aria until my sister was three months into her pregnancy. Believe me, I was shocked. We talked about her plan, so her becoming a single mother wasn't the most surprising part. And, I guess I knew that she had mentioned that she wanted to start a family by age thirty. She'll be thirty-one next month. But, honestly, I thought she'd dropped the idea because she stopped bringing it up."

"I remember you saying before that your sister was left at the altar before her wedding."

"Right. Two years ago. It was pretty awful." He understood that kind of pain on a soul level.

"Is there any chance the two of them reconnected and this could be his child?"

Emery shook her head. "Not the slightest possibility. He's now married to the person from his office that he'd started seeing while he was engaged to my sister."

A betrayal like that didn't go away easily.

"As far as where she got the donor for Aria, my sister went to a place called The Fertility Zone."

"Hold on a second." Eli positioned the laptop facing him. He pulled up a search engine and entered the name of the clinic she'd used. He was pretty certain he'd heard that name before and he couldn't recall why.

He got several hits online. The doctor who ran the clinic had been caught up in a recent scandal and accused of making up donor profiles and using his own sperm when supplies ran low.

"The doctor who runs the place is under indictment." He repositioned the screen so that she could see.

"Oh, no." Emery leaned toward the screen. "This is awful."

"Is it possible your sister knew?" This shed a whole new light on what might be going down.

"I don't see how she could've missed it. It seems to be all over the news and even though my sister has been consumed with this little one, she had to realize this was an issue." She nodded toward the carrier with the sleeping baby in it. "But then honestly, I don't think my sister would care where the donor came from now that she has Aria. She's perfect."

Eli was having a hard time creating a link between this news and her sister's situation unless she found out something that hadn't reached news outlets yet. She could be sitting on information that could bring the doctor down. But how? Why? What would the motive be? This clinic had to have dozens maybe hundreds of clients since it opened five years ago, according to one article. "At the very least, this doctor operates a shady practice."

His cell phone buzzed in his pocket. He fished it out and checked the screen. "It's Ben."

"My car."

Eli nodded as he answered the call. "Thanks for opening your shop on a Sunday, Ben. I owe you a huge favor for this."

"Not that we're keeping score, but I think I'm still in the hole." Ben laughed. The two went way back to middle school when Ben's family first moved to town. Ben was a bear of a kid who'd turned into a teddy bear as an adult. He was one of Eli's favorite people.

"What's the damage?" Eli asked.

"The ignition switch broke down. The good news is that I can fix it in about twenty minutes. The bad news is that I don't have the parts in stock. The place I ordered parts is closed today, which means it will be Monday at the earliest before I can get the part in. How badly does your friend need her car in the next day or so?"

"The faster, the better. As soon as you can have the parts delivered, I'd appreciate an update."

"Not a problem, Eli." One of Ben's five kids yelled for his dad in the background.

"I appreciate you, man." Speaking of which, Eli had been meaning to see if Ben wanted to meet up at the park with his kids one of these Sundays. He'd given Eli advice on child-rearing from a father's perspective and it had proved to be some of the most helpful.

"I'll call as soon as the parts come in. Once I get those in the shop, you might as well head over because I'll be done before you can get here." Ben was the best mechanic in the area and it was easy to see why.

"Sounds like a plan. I'll talk to you later." Eli ended the call and relayed the information to Emery.

"WHAT IF MY SISTER CALLS?" Emery pushed to standing and started pacing around the kitchen. The bigger question was, what if she didn't? But Emery didn't want to voice that. At least not yet. All her hopes were riding on her sister contacting her.

"I'm sure there's a vehicle here on the property that we can lend you. Do you know how to handle driving a truck?"

"I've driven a tour bus, I can handle a truck."

"Remind me to ask you about that later." She turned to face Eli and found a confused look and a raised eyebrow staring back at her.

There were so many things about being on the road back then that made her feel carefree. Being young with no responsibility and early enough in her life that she could get away with 'experiencing life' as Haven had put it before anyone expected her to get a real job. Now, she was a responsible adult with a career track and an apartment. The less-than reliable car was her main setback but she was grateful to have transportation and it worked most of the time. Eli's generosity knew no bounds even though she couldn't accept. "I can't take your truck."

Eli chuckled. "I wasn't offering mine. We have a few spares next to the barn that ranch hands use for picking up hay at the feed store. If one goes missing for a couple of days, no one's going to care or notice. I'll give Dakota a heads-up because he's the one responsible for seeing to repairs and keeping track of where the vehicles are."

"I have no way to pay you back for everything you're doing for me. I don't live in Fort Worth in a big mansion with vehicles to spare. It's just me and my sister, and now Aria. There's no way I can reciprocate." She waved her arms around, realizing she probably sounded a little bit hysterical. She also realized the baby was in the same room, sleeping. At least for now. If Emery kept at it she might wake the little angel. So, she lowered her voice when she said, "This is too much to ask of any one person and especially a stranger."

Eli looked genuinely offended when he folded his arms over a broad chest. "I've told you more about my personal life than I've told anyone, including the people closest to me who I love the most. My brothers. I think we crossed the bridge of friendship a few hours ago. Or at least I hope we did. It may seem strange considering that I've already spilled my guts out to you, but I don't just tell anyone my business. In fact, I never talk about my personal life."

Wow. It changed her perspective when she heard it put that way. Now, she really felt bad. He had shared very personal details about his life and he didn't strike her as the type who blabbered his secrets to anyone let alone someone he barely knew. "It's too late to say I'm sorry. But I can say that I feel bad. That was a jerk move on my part and you didn't deserve it. I'm not used to accepting help. So, I guess that makes me pretty bad at it. If you'll accept my apology, I'd like to ask for your forgiveness."

He sat there for a long moment like he was contemplating his next move. "I want to help you,

Emery. I'm selfish. It feels good to help someone out who can use a hand up. I accept your apology and I also understand why you don't want to feel like you're taking a handout. Hell, I respect you for it because I'm just as stubborn. At least consider my offer. There are no strings attached. I promise that. It really does feel good to help an honest person who has hit a rough patch."

His words spoken with such compassion had her reconsidering. "I'll take you up on your offer on one condition, Eli."

"Name it."

"We figure out some way to let me pay you back once we find my sister and figure out what happened."

"Done."

"Do you promise?" She stared him dead in the eyes. Emery had always had a gift at being able to tell when someone was lying. She'd seen it in her ex the last time he'd told her that he still loved her the same. His life had been changing and she realized he was just hanging on to the past to give himself a sense of normal. She didn't doubt that he loved her. The relationship had morphed into more of a deep friendship and she'd become his support system. It wasn't the kind of romantic love that gave butterflies in her stomach or sparks in his eye. They'd barely been adults when they first got together, and his life had sounded exciting to a kid who'd grown up on the same street without venturing much past her apartment complex.

"I give you my word." With Eli's gaze locked onto hers, a dozen of those butterflies released. One look from him brought out a response she'd never experienced with another man.

"Then, it's a deal." Emery glanced at the clock. It was noon and that meant her sister had disappeared seven hours ago. She walked over to the table and picked up the temporary phone Haven had given her. Still no calls, no messages. "Can I see that laptop?"

Eli repositioned it toward where she'd been sitting moments before. "Be my guest."

"I want to check hospitals in the Fort Worth area just to see if by chance she's there and that's the reason she hasn't called." The dread building in her chest reminded her that Haven would've checked on Aria by now if she was physically capable. Examining Eli's expression, she realized he thought the same thing. As a dad, and a good one at that, he would know.

"Good idea. Something to keep in mind is that she may not have identification on her. So, you'll want to ask if a Jane Doe has arrived, as well."

"Right." He made a good point and yet those words still hurt. She couldn't fathom her sister in some ER being worked on without a name. The hospital staff would care for her just the same, but it meant something to Emery that they would know her sister's name.

She started with the number one hospital for trauma and came up empty. Four calls later, she got a hit.

"A Jane Doe with multiple stab wounds was admitted three hours ago." She blinked dry eyes, wishing that she could just cry and release some of the pent-up frustration and hurt building. "Her description matches my sister's."

7

"We can be there in a few hours." Eli pushed to standing and was confused when Emery sat still, crossing her arms over her chest.

"I can't risk it."

"Why not? What's going on?"

Emery sat there, staring at her cell phone. Her jaw was set and her gaze was steady. The only hint that she might crumble came when her chin quivered.

Then, she blew out a sharp breath. "As I was leaving my apartment complex this morning, a truck with blacked-out windows followed me and gave me a scare. I drove straight to the police station and he followed me until I reached the parking lot."

Eli didn't like the sound of any of this. A person matching her sister's description was in the hospital with multiple stab wounds and Emery had a run-in that she'd kept quiet about? Everything about her situation was tricky, and it was painfully clear that she didn't know who to trust. She didn't know him from Adam, and, to be fair, she had tried to refuse his help, which eased the sting of her possibly putting his children's only parent in danger.

"Did you see the driver? Or if the person had any weapons?"

"He put on his high beams, basically blinding me. There was one point it seemed like he was going to try to whip around me and I was afraid he was going to try to run me off the road. I maneuvered over into the next lane before he could make a move, fully expecting him to ram me from behind. Honestly, I was pretty shocked when he didn't."

"He just backed off? Just like that?"

She was already nodding her head.

Why would he do that? Eli needed to chew on that information for a minute.

"Well, that's interesting." Eli made his way over to the coffee machine and poured another cup. Someone put her sister in the hospital but was careful not to hurt Emery. Why?

"I thought the same thing. I mean, whoever was driving the truck had the perfect chance to run me right off the road. My little hatchback would have been no match for the size of that thing."

"Maybe the person intended to intimidate you all along and not hurt you."

"My mind just keeps going back to one question. Why?" Obviously, it was her sister the person was after.

"It's possible the person thought you were hiding your sister. The jerk might not have realized that she wasn't with you." Again, this is where growing up surrounded by law enforcement kicked his brain into gear. "And it's also a possibility that this person didn't want to hurt your sister."

"Although, now she's probably lying in a hospital bed and fighting for her life." The chin quivered again but she held her head high like she refused to give in.

Granted, they couldn't be absolutely certain without a positive ID that the person in the hospital was her sister. The likelihood that some random person would come in matching her sister's description to a T was slim. Eli wanted to offer some reassurance. He was starting to care more for Emery than was probably smart on his part.

There was something about extreme circumstances that stripped people down to the base of who they really were. In Emery's case, she was intelligent, strong. More so than she gave herself credit for. He could add other words to the list. Brave...

Eli could go on for days about her good qualities but there were other things to consider right now. His mind snapped back the investigation. "I'm processing everything I know so far. Your sister asked you not to go to law enforcement. She could have taken Aria to a friend or coworker, but she brought her to you. That has to mean something."

"She trusts me, for one."

He nodded. "But she also put you in danger as well as Aria."

"She never would've done that on purpose."

"Not if she had another option. Do any of your sister's friends have an issue with her? Or had she been in a fight with anyone recently?"

"No one that she told me about. She would sometimes grumble about this or that person at work. But she'd been so detached from office gossip and politics since the last trimester of her pregnancy. All she really ever talked about was being excited for Aria. She made lists of all the things she needed to do to get ready for the baby. She complained about how huge she felt and how swollen her ankles were. She talked about a deep craving for vanilla ice cream and watermelon. I'm pretty sure I was cutting one up every few days in the last weeks leading up to the birth." Emery smiled at the memory and it brightened her face.

Eli walked over to her and put his hand on her shoulder. "I'll do everything in my power to make sure your sister survives. Baby Aria needs her mother." Haven may not have been talking about work problems, but that didn't mean they didn't exist. "First thing in the morning, I'd like to visit her office and ask a few questions of her coworkers. I can't stress enough how important I think it is at this point to bring in the law and especially considering your sister's condition."

Emery was already shaking her head before he finished his sentence. "I agree that going to her office and talking to her coworkers is a good idea. But she was clear about not bringing in the law, and I have to respect her wishes."

Emery's loyalty was admirable. He had to consider that bringing in the law would make matters worse for her sister. Only Haven knew for certain and it wasn't like they could ask her. But he also needed to make sure that Haven had protection while she was in a vulnerable state. Whoever put her in the hospital might return to finish the job. "I'm sending a security detail to the hospital to watch over your sister."

Shocked didn't begin to describe the expression on Emery's face as she looked up at him while he picked up his phone and made the call to have someone assigned as security.

The second call he made was to the hospital to let them know he was sending a 'family' member to watch over a patient. When he finished the second conversation, he heard footsteps coming from down the hallway.

A glance at the clock said it was lunchtime. Emery was about to meet the family.

Emery had gone to plenty of places and met more people than she could count. However, her stomach was in knots at the thought of meeting Eli's family. It was strange to care so much about what people she'd never met thought about her.

Her mind still reeled from finding out the news about her sister and she was waiting eagerly for details about Haven's condition. It had to be her sister in that hospital bed. Her description was spot on and it explained why Haven hadn't reached out since this morning.

Still, it was impossible to think someone could intentionally hurt her sister. Emery's heavy thoughts were interrupted by the sound of footsteps.

A tall man who resembled Eli came into the room.

"Emery, this is my brother, Cayden. He recently returned home after spending most of his life as one of the most successful trackers in the U.S."

Cayden was tall and built, similar to Eli. To her taste, Eli was the better looking one of the two. It was easy to see that they were related with their dark hair and light blue eyes. This family had the kind of bone structure people dreamed of and magazines exploited.

"Nice to meet you, Cayden." She stood and took his outstretched hand, noting his firm grip. She couldn't help but think this was exactly the kind of family she would want to have her back in an emergency. If the other brothers were anything like these two, they'd have no problem stepping up and would be more than capable of handling anyone or anything that came their way.

Cayden's brows were drawn together, and he smiled through concern lines bracketing his mouth.

Eli seemed to catch on immediately. "Is everything okay? Where's Madison?"

"She's feeling more tired than usual today. She's having more of those early contractions and they seem to be taking the wind out of her." Cayden looked to his brother. "The doc says this is all normal, but he wants her to come in first thing tomorrow morning."

"Sorry to hear she's uncomfortable. The last month seems to be the hardest. I know Madison is ready to be done at this point." Eli's assessment was met with a nod.

Cayden's gaze shifted to Aria. Emery was grateful he didn't load the two of them up with questions. Heaven knew he could have. For one, he'd walked into his family's kitchen to a stranger and an infant, but then again, Eli had mentioned that no one would be too surprised by her presence on the ranch. Folks in Fort Worth were polite, but she felt the Quinn family took hospitality to a whole new level.

Much to her surprise, after spending years of her life needing to be on the road, being in a place like

Quinnland was a nice change of pace. There was something about the warmth between the brothers that was palpable that made the place feel cozy. And even though the main house was bigger than she could ever imagine, the space was filled with an air of love.

"Her doctor said to head straight on to the hospital if the pain got worse. Problem is, she keeps putting up a brave front with me and that makes it hard to tell just how much she's suffering." Cayden trained his gaze on the baby and a slight smile upturned the corners of his lips.

As if on cue, Aria stirred. She took in a couple of quick breaths, the signal she was working up to cry. "She's probably hungry. And I need to change her. Can anyone point me to a good place?"

"I got this." Cayden motioned for her to follow him. She shot a quick look toward Eli, who was already getting out the formula from her diaper bag. The men's movements were that of a well-oiled machine.

"Do you mind?" Cayden nodded toward the baby carrier. "I need all the practice I can get."

"Be my guest." Emery smiled. She couldn't help herself. She and her sister had always been close but this took sibling connection to a whole new level. She and Haven could learn a few things from the Quinn brothers and she could only pray they'd have the chance.

Again, her sister's condition brought a wave of fear.

Emery did her level best to keep her emotions in check. Keeping a positive mental attitude was a lifeline in hard situations and had kept her sane when life had dished out more than she thought she could handle.

Eli's brother led her down the hall to a room that looked like it used to be an office. Instead of wood flooring like in so much of the downstairs, there were special floors. They were soft and spongy when she walked. There were toys scattered around and in bins. To one side of the room was a baby changing station.

Aria started a soft cry and Emery could tell that her niece was winding up to an even bigger one.

"I can take her off your hands," she offered.

Cayden handed over the carrier, which Emery immediately set down before unbuckling the straps.

"I wasn't around much when Oliver and Olivia were this tiny. She looks like it would be easy to break her." It was endearing to see someone so strong and otherwise confident admit to his own vulnerability.

"She's tougher than she looks."

"You're good with her," he said.

She thanked him. "Aria doesn't have a father to speak of and I'm not the best judge, considering mine took off when I wasn't much older than her. But if you're even half the dad your brother is, and I bet you will be, you'll do just fine." Emery hadn't given much thought to having children of her own. She figured if she met the right person and it happened, great. If not, she didn't feel like there would be something missing in her life. An annoying little voice in the back of her mind told her that wasn't quite true. After being with Eli and seeing him around his kids, she had a random thought or two about what it would be like to be with him, to make a family with him. And since she couldn't figure out where the heck that thought came from, she tucked it away and tried to forget about it.

"I appreciate your confidence. I'm sure I'll be on sea legs in the beginning. Eventually, I'll get the hang of it."

"These guys grow fast. I know she seems tiny to you now. You should've seen her five and a half weeks ago." Emery kept the conversation going while she moved over to the changing table. She'd already grabbed a diaper from the bag before leaving the kitchen. It was good to have something to keep her hands busy and her mind from spinning out over the fact that her sister was lying in a hospital bed in the ER more than three hours' drive away.

Aria's diaper was wet, so nothing too shocking if Cayden wasn't used to seeing a diaper changed. He hovered at the door and seemed interested in what she was doing. He also kept his distance and she had to stifle a chuckle. She'd been the same way when Aria was first born, worrying that she needed to give the newborn some privacy.

Six weeks later, she was starting to feel like a

veteran. Of course, being left alone with her niece had knocked her back a few steps because she realized just how ill-equipped she was at caring for Aria alone.

Cayden brought his forearm up and leaned against the doorjamb. "It does seem like just yesterday my niece and nephew were born. And now, I'm about to be a father myself."

"You seem pretty tough to me. I think you can handle the job." Confidence was huge in the first few weeks of handling a baby. She'd figured it out the hard way by having zero.

"Sometimes, people who seem strong on the outside aren't as tough as we might think they are," he said after a thoughtful pause.

Suddenly, she got the impression they weren't talking about him anymore.

"You seem like a nice person and I'm certain to be stepping way out of my bounds here," he said and then paused for a few beats before continuing. "When it comes to protecting my brother, I'd rather say I'm sorry than ask permission."

"Okay." Emery stayed focused on the task at hand, not risking a glance at Cayden. She didn't want to give away the vulnerability she felt toward Eli or the connection that sizzled as much as it comforted, and she was pretty certain her emotions were written all over her face.

Chin to her chest, she replaced the old diaper,

cleaned off Aria's bottom and then situated a new one. She peeled back the tape and secured the diaper as she listened.

"It doesn't show, but he's had a rough time of it. He loves those kiddos more than anything and focusing on them has gotten him through a dark time. I know he seems okay on the outside. And we'll all make sure that he is. Here's the thing, he never talks about it with us. As far as I know, he never talks about what he went through with anyone."

Hearing it from Cayden made her even more grateful Eli had decided to confide in her. It also made her feel special. "Can I ask a question?"

"Shoot." Cayden chuckled. "I'm pretty sure we just moved beyond polite conversation."

"I just met Eli. Why are you telling me all this?"

"Because I've never seen him look at another woman the way he looks at you. And that includes his ex."

Emery's hands trembled as she picked up Aria and held the baby to her chest. She wished that her face didn't give away every last bit of her emotions. She'd always been that way. Emery couldn't count the number of times her mother had said she wore her emotions on her sleeve.

"Thank you for telling me. But I'm going back to my life in Fort Worth as soon as I can."

"Fort Worth?"

"Yes. Your brother had the same reaction when I brought up my city. What does he have against Fort Worth?"

"That's where his ex is from." Cayden stepped into the hallway to make room for her to pass. "Do you want me to grab the carrier?"

"Do you mind?" she asked.

"Not a bit. I can see that your hands are full already." Was he still talking about the carrier? "Just in case you don't end up going home to Fort Worth, you should know that he's one of the best."

She probably shouldn't admit this. "I figured that out on my own." After a couple of steps into the hallway, she paused and then turned around. "For the record, I'm going home."

Cayden didn't respond. Instead, he grinned ear-to-ear.

8

The hum of voices could be heard from down the hall. Emery would be intimidated under normal circumstances. It was probably just how warm Eli and Cayden had been that had her nerves settled well below panic. She also reminded herself that Haven was in the hospital, under protection, and getting the care she needed to survive.

Cayden's warning flashed in her mind as she neared the kitchen. She couldn't fault him for wanting to protect his brother. Heck, his consideration and concern for Eli had only served to warm her heart and endear her to the family even more. It was easy to see how close the brothers were, and she imagined the other five were just the same.

The squawk of a police radio stopped her in her tracks.

"Are you okay?" Cayden stopped, too.

"Yes. Fine." Except that she could hear the shakiness in her own voice. Eli wouldn't do that to her. He would not go behind her back and call in law enforcement. "Who is that? Who's here?"

"A few of my brothers and their wives. I'm sure Oliver and Olivia are up by now. Marianne will be in there. That's the reason for the amazing smell. She's a great cook."

She waited a second for him to continue. He didn't. She had to fight the urge to turn down the opposite hallway and run.

"Is that a police radio?" She asked the question in as calm a voice as she could muster, considering how hard her heart pounded against her ribs.

"That would belong to our cousin, Griff. He's the sheriff." Emery was certain based on Cayden's casual tone that he hadn't picked up on the fact that she was terrified of running into law enforcement. A guy paid to notice things wasn't exactly the kind of person she wanted around right now.

"I didn't know your cousin was a sheriff."

Cayden's brows knitted together. "I'm sorry. I assumed you knew. Everyone knows our family..." It seemed to dawn on him that she wasn't from around there. "Right. Do you want me to grab my brother?"

"No. It's fine." She figured it might make her look suspect if she avoided his cousin. Besides, based on the number of voices she heard it wasn't like she would be alone in a room with him. She played her hesitation off. "I'm a fish out of water around groups of new people."

Cayden leaned toward her. "I apologize for putting you on the spot a few minutes ago. I promise all the others have better manners than mine."

Gathering her courage, she smiled. "You don't have to apologize to me for looking out for your brother." No one could ever mean those words more than she did.

"Are you ready to meet the others?"

Emery blew out a breath. "Ready as I'll ever be."

Walking into the room, the first thing that hit her was the similarities among the brothers. Their cousin had sandy-blond hair but had a similar height and build. The calendar joke came to mind. They could raise a lot of money for charity because people would line up to buy a copy.

Eli spotted her from across the room and made a beeline toward her. He stood next to her and put a reassuring hand on the small of her back. Contact sent volts of electric currents rippling through her.

Cayden's comments resurfaced. Was it possible Eli felt the same way when the two of them touched? She was certain she'd seen something pass behind his eyes when she'd touched his hand earlier.

Eli introduced her to the table full of people as he

handed her a bottle of formula for Aria. Emery would never remember all the names of the brothers and their fiancées or wives, but she couldn't help but think how nice it would be to have so much family surrounding her. Aria quieted the minute she tasted her formula.

Emery did her level best not to stare at Griff or give away the panic she felt being in the same room with the sheriff.

Thankfully, Eli excused them and took her and the baby outside.

The backyard was beyond anything she'd seen, but she wasn't there for the view. "You didn't tell me your cousin was the sheriff."

"It never came up."

She must've shot him a look because he added, "There's a lot that we don't know about each other's families. I didn't realize Griff was coming over for lunch today. As you might have already guessed, people come and go here."

Emery gently rocked Aria mostly to give herself something to help release some of the pent-up energy she felt. "I'm not exactly in the right frame of mind to be around the law."

"You don't have to be. Lunch won't last that long and no one will be shocked if I give you a tour of the barn. My cousin will most likely be gone by the time we return to the main house." Eli held his hands up in the surrender position, palms out. "I give you my word that I didn't know he was coming."

There was so much sincerity in his voice and honesty in his eyes. She believed him without a doubt. "You're doing a lot for me and my sister. I want you to know how much I appreciate it."

"I have a feeling you'd do the same thing for anyone you cared about." Those words had a similar effect as his touch, spreading warmth through her.

She didn't remind him of the fact that he did that for a stranger. And she couldn't deny the connection she felt to him. His brother was probably right to warn her. But he was wrong about one thing. She doubted that she had the influence to hurt Eli. However, as much as she felt drawn to him already, she realized how much trouble she'd be in if she let her feelings run rampant. He'd have the power to shatter her.

Aria finished her bottle and Emery gently repositioned the little girl on her shoulder. She patted Aria's back, satisfied with herself for remembering this time.

There was something magical about being around Eli. He had the power to calm her and make her feel like everything would work out despite the stark circumstances.

Taking in a deep breath, she turned toward the barn and the mass of land beyond. "I can see why you would stick around here. This place is beyond anything I've ever seen."

"There's nothing quite like staring up at a wide-open summer sky."

"Light blue is my favorite. It reminds me a lot of the color of your eyes." Again, she turned her face away from him so she wouldn't give away the fact she was blushing.

Eli's cell phone buzzed. He fished it out of his pocket and checked the screen. With a look of surprise, he glanced up and said, "T.J. is home."

"We should get back inside." Emery had already turned toward the house and started walking. She paused and turned around when he didn't follow.

"Are you coming?" she asked.

Eli should want to pit stop in the house and see his father. So why was he hesitating?

There was something about being out here on the ranch with Emery that made the world seem complete. The feeling confused him as much as it intrigued him. The surprising fact was that he was enjoying her company more than he cared to admit. He was a little bit more than frustrated at himself for letting his emotions run away with him.

But, what could he say? She was intelligent, caring and beautiful. The total package.

This was a case of the right person coming along at the wrong time. He had no energy left for a relationship and no time. Relationships, he'd learn the hard way, couldn't exactly be put on autopilot. It took work and effort on both people's parts. And, honestly, he couldn't imagine fitting one more thing into his already busy day.

Of course, he took note of the love and care Emery gave to her niece. Her protective streak over her sister and Aria ran miles long. He couldn't help but admire her commitment to the people she loved. It had been one of the many qualities missing in his ex. Looking back, he and Camille rarely ever talked about things that really mattered, like family and responsibility. In fact, the first hint of duty had sent her running for the door.

Not Emery. But he didn't want to notice those qualities in her that made his pulse quicken and his chest squeeze. It probably reminded him a little too much of what had been missing with Camille.

Funny fact was that he'd had no idea he'd been missing out until meeting Emery. When it came to her, words like 'long-haul' came to mind. He was torn between the feeling that he could fall for her and the reality that a long-term relationship probably wasn't in the cards for him right now and maybe ever after how far south his last relationship had gone.

With a sharp sigh, he said, "Right behind you."

Before they walked up the back porch steps, he put one hand on her shoulder to stop her. "Do you want me to take my cousin aside and ask him if he's ever heard of the doctor or clinic that your sister used?" There'd been something he couldn't pinpoint niggling at the back of his mind. He could only hope it would come to him before it was too late.

The sheer panic on Emery's face when she turned around gave him his answer.

"That's why I'm asking first. I want you to know that I would never break a promise or tell anyone about your situation without consulting you first." He meant that, too.

The tension lines in her face relaxed a little bit, hearing his promise. "Thank you. This whole situation is stressful enough without adding to it." She raked her top teeth over her bottom lip, a nervous tick he'd noticed. She also did it when she was listening to him and he hoped he was getting through because Griff could prove to be a valuable asset in an investigation. He had resources at his disposal they didn't.

"On second thought, as long as no names are mentioned and you ask him cousin-to-cousin, I don't see the harm." The signs that Emery was beginning to trust Eli came through loud and clear.

He offered a genuine smile in return. Her honey-gold eyes glittered with what he recognized as need. A thunderclap of desire reverberated through him. There was so much unspoken chemistry between them it was almost unreal. Touching her creamy skin only made him want to run his fingers up the nape of her neck and around her jawline to her full pink lips. Lips that he wanted to taste more than anything in that moment.

Standing on the bottom step, she was near enough to his height for him to do just that. She leaned toward him and planted a soft, tender kiss against his mouth. Eli had never felt so much power and so much passion in one kiss, and all he could think was, *more*.

Since this wasn't the time or the place, he pulled back enough to lock gazes with her. "I'll take a rain check on that kiss."

She smiled and more of those flames brightened her cheeks.

"And for the record, that's about the sexiest thing I've ever seen." His admission was met with an even bigger smile. He could hear the huskiness in his own voice. This time, her smile even reached her eyes. The spark there was as undeniable as sunshine in a Texas summer. Both were hot.

"Since we're keeping score now, you're not so bad yourself." She turned toward the back door and then took the next couple of steps, leaving him standing there a little out of breath from the kiss and the moment happening between them. *Way to keep in check, Quinn. Nice job.*

Time to face the music and find out what T.J. had been up to. Eli stepped around Emery in time to open the back door for her. He could use the excuse that her hands were full but he also liked doing things for her, even little things like opening doors. She was so different than Camille who'd expected Eli to open every door and treat her like a princess. Being from Texas, that kind of courtesy was ingrained in him. There was a little less pleasure in doing it for someone who took it for granted.

There was a musical quality to her voice when she thanked him this time. He was close enough to want to capture the freckle just above her lip with his mouth. There were a few other temptations when it came to her, too. Like the kisses he'd like to place on her temples, her eyelids, her chin as he worked his way back to those pouty pink lips of hers.

And since all of that was about as likely as getting milk from a bee, he gave himself a mental headshake. It had been a really long time since he met a woman who had that kind of power over him. The pull toward Emery was a thousand times stronger than that of his ex's, and he'd married her.

He'd also been burned, and hopefully learned.

Trailing behind Emery into his family's kitchen, the low hum of chatter struck him first. It was almost impossible to believe his entire family could be under one roof. He never thought he'd see the day when Aiden would come home, let alone his baby brother, Phoenix.

Eli was hit square in the chest and almost knocked him back a step with emotion. Looking around the room, all he could think was that this scene was pretty great if anyone asked him. Seeing his kids seated at the table with everyone he loved choked him up. He cleared his throat to unclog the emotion.

He led Emery over to the table and toward Oliver and Olivia. The second his daughter spotted him, she squealed with delight.

"Hey, sweet girl." He leaned down and kissed her on the forehead.

Oliver clapped, smile, and said, "Dadda."

Whatever was left of Eli's heart became liquid in that moment. Nope, he couldn't regret the heartache he'd experienced when his ex had walked out. Not when he got two of the most perfect children in the world out of the deal.

"Where is he?" Eli asked his brother Noah. "Where's T.J."

"Said he wanted to change into something more comfortable. We already put in a call to Phoenix, who is on his way." Their youngest brother owned and operated a string of the best burrito food trucks in Texas. He'd decided to stay in Austin while expecting a baby with his new wife. He was the only brother living outside of Gunner.

"Did you see him?" Eli's curiosity was getting the better of him.

"Yes, I did, and he looked the same as when he left." Noah's response wasn't unexpected. Eli had done a pretty good job of not being on pins and needles about his father's announcement—an announcement that had everyone worried no matter how much they played it off.

Each of Eli's brothers had now come home and speculation was running wild about what the big news could be. A man like T.J. didn't retire. The thought of T.J. being sick didn't sit right when he seemed as healthy as ever. The man could be taking stock of his life. Eli had heard of that happening with men T.J.'s age.

Eli glanced around. "Where's Marianne?"

Noah wiggled his eyebrows. "She went to check on our father and gather Dakota."

Eli made a note to ask Noah about that later. Right now, he couldn't help but notice the easy way in which his sisters-in-law, Gina and Mikayla, had taken to Emery. They were currently 'oohing' and 'aahing' over Aria.

Madison was the only one missing, but not for long. She walked...no, *walked* wasn't quite the right word for how she entered the room. It was more like a waddle. She smiled and nodded at Eli as she made a beeline for her husband. Her gaze stopped briefly at Emery.

If Madison was surprised, she didn't show it. She stopped halfway across the room and put the flat of her hand on her lower back. Her face scrunched up like she was in pain. Cayden was out of his chair and to her side in a heartbeat. He helped her to the table and then the chair he'd occupied a few moments ago.

Everyone continued chatting, but all eyes had shifted to Madison.

"Do you want anything? Water?" Stress carved lines in Cayden's forehead.

"Maybe just some ice." Madison had that pregnancy glow, despite her obvious discomfort.

"I'll get it, man." Eli motioned for Cayden to stay by Madison's side.

"Thank you." Cayden took her hand in his.

"I'll be okay in a few minutes. This is a tough one," she said to him as Eli filled a glass with ice and brought it over to her.

Before she had a chance to say anything, T.J. entered the kitchen. All conversation stopped and all gazes averted to him. Marianne shuffled in behind him. The fact that she didn't meet anyone's gaze caused a lump of dread to form in Eli's stomach. Honest to a fault, she'd never been one to hide or lie.

Eli braced himself for bad news.

And then all attention went to Madison who grunted in pain and grabbed onto Cayden's arm like he was the last man on a raft and she stood on a ship that was going under.

"Ohmygod, I think my water just broke."

9

"We need to get to the hospital. *Now*." Those words from Madison were met with the kind of organized chaos of a fire drill in an elementary school.

Eli figured staying at home and tending to the main house should fall to him as everyone else kicked into high gear. He needed to stay with Oliver and Olivia. And then there was Emery and Aria to consider.

Cayden stayed by Madison's side as Noah volunteered to get his vehicle and drive. A pair of sisters-in-law volunteered to grab clothing since Madison said nothing was packed.

The place ran like a well-oiled machine with everyone pitching in.

"I'll go to the hospital." T.J.'s declaration was met

with a few nods. This softer side of T.J. was going to take some getting used to. Eli liked it, though.

"I'll stay here to help with the littles," Marianne said.

Eli cocked an eyebrow. It wasn't that Marianne wasn't great with the kiddos. She was. In fact, there was no one quite like her. Eli had probably leaned on her too much since his ex had walked out. Not that Marianne had minded. She'd done what any good grandparent would do, rolled up her sleeves and volunteered her services.

In fact, she'd devoted a good part of her life to the Quinn family. Eli figured it was high time she had something for herself. And he noticed when a look passed between her and Dakota. He left it at that. He was not one to judge what other people did or didn't do. But he did wonder if there was something going on between the two of them.

"I'll be at the bunkhouse if anybody needs me." With that, Dakota exited out the back door. The entire room cleared in less than five minutes.

"I'll keep you posted," Noah promised.

In addition to taking care of the littles and helping Emery figure out what happened to her sister, Eli could set up a command post at the main house. Madison might be having false contractions. He remembered what that was like from when his ex had gone through labor for the first time. The second child had come faster, cutting her labor time in half. Considering that Madison wasn't due for another few weeks, he figured they might keep her overnight for observation and then send her home tomorrow.

Unless her water really had broken. That was a whole different path.

Granted, he was no doctor and from what he could gather every pregnancy was different. Even so, he'd heard his ex's obstetrician mention a few times that labor tended to run long in first-time pregnancies.

"I hope Madison is okay. Your family has been amazing to me and it would be impossible not to care what happened to them." Emery was holding onto Aria like there was no tomorrow.

"She'll be in good hands at the hospital. She has the best doctor and medical team. Fingers crossed everything goes according to plan, meaning she'll be sent home to rest for her last couple of weeks." Eli didn't figure this was the time to mention that his father had donated a wing to the hospital in his wife's name after her death. Madison would get top-notch care.

Marianne returned to the kitchen. "Are either of you guys hungry?"

"I can get something for us," Eli said, and then realized she most likely wanted something to do to keep busy.

"How about Oliver and Olivia? They've already

napped and eaten. How about I take them into the playroom?" She looked at Emery. "I'd be happy to take your little angel, as well."

Apparently, Marianne didn't see the look on Emery's face or the determination with which she held Aria.

"Thank you for the offer. I think she might feel better being in here with me," Emery quickly said.

"Well, if you change your mind, I'll be in the playroom with these two little darlings. Your angel is welcome anytime." Marianne brought over a washcloth and washed Oliver and then Olivia's face before taking them out of the room.

Eli wasn't sure what he would've done without Marianne for the past year and a half. She'd been a godsend to him and his children, and he couldn't imagine life at the ranch without her.

Which had him concerned. She'd been acting strange lately, distant. He couldn't quite put his finger on it but dread swirled in his gut at the thought that she might want to retire. She deserved it, though. Marianne deserved the best and he'd support any decision she made.

As willing as she had been to step in and care for his children, it was time for her to have a life of her own. Even Eli could see that. So, after the scare with Madison settled down and T.J. delivered his big news, Eli intended to make a priority out of finding suitable live-in help. No matter how much Marianne would protest, and she would, he needed to give her that freedom. As long as she believed he needed him on a day-to-day, she would never claim her independence.

"Since my cousin took off with the others, I didn't exactly get a chance to talk to him about the clinic. What do you want to do next?" he asked Emery.

She bit back a yawn. "I had to help my sister with paying her bills once. I feel like if I could get to my own laptop that I could log on to her accounts. If there was something weird going on, I have to think there would be deposits or payments. There should be some kind of trail. We should be able to track down where she's been and what she's been doing. Right?"

"It's possible," he said. "Any chance you have access to her email?"

"Yes. As a matter of fact, I do."

Eli walked over to the table and positioned the laptop where Emery had been seated. She placed Aria in her carrier, where the happy little girl blew spit bubbles and tried to reach up to the toys attached to the handle, dangling down. At six weeks old, her eyes were just beginning to focus and her hand-eye coordination was lacking in the most adorable way.

Emery took a seat in front of the laptop and then pulled up her sister's email.

"Your sister either has her cell phone or her email attached to her bank password if she's set up like most accounts. If it's her cell phone, were out of luck since we have no idea where that is. But a lot of times people link to their email, in which case you can click on the button that says forgot password and reset it." Before he finished his sentence, Emery was already rocking her head. She was quick and had already caught on to where he was headed with this.

"Tomorrow can't come soon enough for me," she began. "I'd like to talk to a couple of her coworkers in person and gauge their reactions to whether or not she had any trouble brewing at work. I've traveled all around the country and have met tons of people. I've gotten pretty good at figuring out whether or not people are being honest."

"It's all in the eyes and the body language," he agreed. Most people were easy to read. Eli considered himself good at it. Except when it came to love. That seemed to come with blinders. Even he'd been fooled once. As much as it had burned, he had to admit the worst part was the fact his kids would grow up without their mother. His concern for Oliver and Olivia far outweighed his personal feelings about his marriage. Was that strange?

He had to believe somewhere down deep that he'd realized that him and his ex weren't exactly the best fit. There'd been a few signs along the way. All of which he'd ignored, deciding to let his heart take the wheel.

And even though he'd loved his ex, she didn't stir

up the kind of feelings in him that Emery did. Losing her would be a real loss. And he was determined to figure out a way for the two of them to remain in touch once this situation with her sister was all said and done.

There was something special about Emery. Between being there for his kids and taking care of the ranch, he would have no time to figure out just what it was and that fact shouldn't be as big of a knife stab to the chest as it felt.

Eli figured all it did was prove he was human and capable of falling for someone again. He'd take it as a positive.

"Well, this is strange." The sound of her voice broke through his revelry. Emery pointed toward the screen and slowly scrolled. "See here."

Being this close to her, he breathed in her unique mixture of sunshine and spring flower scent. Under the circumstances, his body's reaction was about as appropriate as sinning in church.

"I don't see anything out of the ordinary." Eli focused all of his attention on the screen and away from thoughts that would lead him down a dead-end road.

"Exactly. I went all the way back to the time when my sister would have gotten pregnant with Aria and there's nothing here. No checks to the doctor. No checks to the clinic."

"She might've used a credit card."

"I already thought of that. She pays her credit card bill directly from her checking account once a month. And when I pulled up her payments, there isn't a significant increase. Wouldn't there be something to show payment to the clinic?"

"There should be. This kind of service doesn't come cheap."

"I mean, I'd have to check her credit card records just to be certain. But I'm not seeing a bump in her expenses until after the baby came, and then that was basically the extra amount she was spending on diapers and formula since she couldn't breastfeed."

The 'thing' that had been niggling at the back of Eli's mind clicked. "That's why the truck didn't hit you. Aria was in the car. Whoever is behind this didn't want to risk hurting her."

Emery leaned back in her chair and folded her arms over her chest, a hurt look darkening her features. "I can't believe my sister lied to me."

"I'm sorry." He of all people knew what it was like to have someone he trusted be dishonest. "It's possible she thought that she was protecting you."

Emery's gaze narrowed. She stared at a spot beyond the laptop on the wall. She was silent for a long moment. "She would've known that I can handle pretty much anything. My guess is that she was protecting Aria's real father."

A WHOLE NEW set of options opened with the revelation that Haven could be protecting Aria's father. Eli had made a great point. Emery had been confused as to why the truck had stopped before hitting her. Someone might be trying to get to Aria. Or take her away. Either way, the person wanted her safe.

"My first thought, sadly, is that maybe my sister got into a relationship with someone at work and he had to protect his reputation."

"I don't know Haven, so I hope you won't take offense at the suggestion. But it seems possible the person she was protecting could've been married."

"That was my first thought, too." Haven wasn't the type to get involved with a married man knowingly. "Aria's father could've lied to my sister and told her he was separated from his wife or getting a divorce. She could've been played."

Eli was already rocking his head in agreement. It seemed their thoughts were running along the same track.

"Believe me when I say people can be convincing." The look on his face and the fact that she knew about his background reminded her that he was speaking from experience.

He wasn't alone. The saying, *Fool me once shame on you but fool me twice and the shame is on me,* came to mind. It was also the reason trusting someone else didn't come naturally to Emery.

With Eli, though, something told her he would move heaven and earth before he would be dishonest with her or anyone else. The man hadn't broken his promise and she had put him to the test.

There was another thing she'd noticed. Eyes always seemed to give people's intentions away. He had a rare mix of serious and clear blue eyes that were beautiful. She could look into his eyes for days. Eyes like those wouldn't lie.

A thought struck Emery. Now that she really thought about it, it was odd how many times Haven had brought up the fertility clinic by name or emphasized who the doctor in charge had been. Thinking back, her sister hadn't even brought up the name of her OB as much and he'd cared for her during her pregnancy and then delivered Aria. It had struck her as odd more than once. She'd ignored her instincts and she couldn't help but wonder if the mistake was costing her sister dearly. Emery should have realized something was going on. "I wish I would've found a way to convince my sister to confide in me."

"Granted, the situation looks bad. You won't get an argument from me on that. On the other hand, I'm sure she had her reasons. To her, they probably even seemed like good ones." Eli's cell phone buzzed. He picked it up and checked the screen. "I better take this. It's my security guard at the hospital."

Emery sat ramrod straight, listening to every word for any sign of what this call might be about. Eli repeated *uh-huh* and *I see* a few times before thanking the caller for the update. He looked at her and seemed to be searching for the right words.

"I'm a big girl. Don't candy-coat anything. What's going on?"

"Your sister is in a medically-induced coma." The sentence was delivered with compassion and she appreciated that. She figured she could take just about any news at this point as long as her sister was alive, and yet his response still caught her off guard as she brought up her hand to cover her gasp.

"The doctor is hopeful for a full recovery. She has lost a lot of blood and was given a transfusion. The doc was able to stitch up her wounds and he said she was strong. She experienced some head trauma. So, he's waiting to see if any swelling occurs on the brain. The next twenty-four hours are critical."

Emery pushed off the table, got to her feet, and started pacing.

Snapping her fingers, she needed to figure out how to get to the hospital unseen. Was that even possible? Would whoever did this to her sister be watching? Waiting for her to show with Aria?

"I think I know what you're about to say and try to

do, and I want to caution you against it. My guy said there was a male wearing a hoodie who turned into the hallway toward your sister's room a few minutes ago. As soon as he got a look at my security detail, he bolted down the stairs."

Didn't that news send a chill rippling up her spine. "What if it was Aria's father?"

"You think maybe she got in a relationship with someone who was bad news?" He quirked a brow.

"It just doesn't sound like my sister. Do you think it could be possible that Aria's father found out about Haven in the hospital and decided to check for himself?"

"Yes. He could be listed as her ICE on her phone," he stated.

Emery's eyebrow shot up this time, a reflex. "What does that mean?"

"In case of emergency. It's the contact we're supposed to list for law enforcement or emergency personnel."

"That's probably me. And she may not have had her cell phone with her. Ditching mine was the first thing she did after she dropped off Aria at my house. I woke up to learn that she'd exchanged my cell phone for the temporary one."

"Right," he said. "Whoever was after her probably had a way to track her using her cell phone and she feared this person could track you the same way."

The phones were most likely gone for good. Being without her cell caused her chest to squeeze.

"Staying on the Aria's father train of thought, maybe he went to check on her because he was concerned but when he saw someone there he freaked out." She also had to consider that he could be the person who would put her there in the first place.

"If it was him, I hope he was there to make sure she was okay. But how would he know where she was in the first place if he wasn't involved?" His question slammed into her.

Emery was gutted at the thought someone her sister trusted could have been the one to put her in the hospital.

10

"I can pull up Haven's social media page on the computer. I don't have passwords to it, but we could skim through her photos and friends to see if anyone looks familiar." Emery pointed toward the laptop's screen.

Eli nodded, thinking that was a good place to start. He checked his phone again and saw that he had a couple of messages from Liam and Isaac. His twin brothers had moments where it seemed like they had the exact same thought at the exact same time. The texts had shown up within minutes of each other and said that Madison was being admitted overnight for observation.

"How is she?" Emery asked.

"How did you know who the texts were about?" He

glanced at her and realized that she'd been studying him.

"Good guess." She shrugged noncommittal but the small smile trying to break through at the corners of her mouth gave away the fact that she was pleased with herself.

"She's doing as well as can be expected at this stage. Looks like she won an overnight stay."

"I remember how tough that last month was for my sister. The last two weeks she was on bed rest and she seemed pretty miserable. For a good cause, though." She glanced over at Aria who was still entertaining herself.

"Aria is a good baby. She and your sister are lucky to have you." Eli couldn't imagine what he would've done without Marianne. To say he'd felt like a fish out of water in those first few weeks after his wife had left him was a lot like saying coffee beans were brown.

"She really is good. I don't know about the lucky part. I haven't been alone with her for a full twenty-four hours and I can't imagine doing any of this without you." Again, she brought her hand over to his.

This time, he linked their fingers. She leaned toward him and he brought his free hand up to cup her chin. Her silky skin was smooth against his calloused fingers. His gaze dropped to those full pink lips of hers. Instinct took over as she positioned her legs in between his thighs. He brought her mouth toward his, wanting to cover that freckle with a kiss.

A thought struck. Was she simply reaching for comfort in a stressful time? Or could there be more between them than temporary? Eli wasn't thrilled to be having this internal conversation with himself, but after what happened with Camille trusting anyone else's intentions wouldn't come naturally.

When Emery's gaze lifted to meet his, her desire came through loud and clear. It would be so easy to lean forward a couple more inches and claim that mouth of hers, which was exactly what Eli planned to do.

The tap, tap, tap of little feet was followed by Marianne's voice. "Here comes the pony."

Oliver's squeal made it all the way into the kitchen before he did. The interruption was probably for the best because kissing Emery would lead him down a slippery slope best avoided.

Eli cleared his throat and stood up. He needed to walk it off and grab a fresh cup of coffee. The temptation to go down that road with Emery, the one that had him acting on their mutual attraction, was strong. It probably wasn't a good call to make right now.

"I'll take some of that coffee if you're offering." Emery had busied herself with Aria.

"Two cups coming right up." About that time, Oliver came bolting through the kitchen. That kid's laugh came straight down from the heavens. "Hey, little guy. Slow down there."

Oliver ran straight to Eli's legs. The little guy practically threw himself against his father's shins and then wrapped his little arms around Eli's knees as best he could.

His round cheeks were flush, his eyes big, his smile wide. Oliver was one of the happiest toddlers Eli had ever witnessed. It warmed his heart, because he thought maybe he wasn't going to mess the kid's life up completely. A face that happy had to mean Eli was doing something right.

Just like a tornado, Oliver turned in the opposite direction and ran back toward the sound of Marianne's voice.

"He's a cute kid. Happy." Those few words from Emery shouldn't be so reassuring to Eli. He shouldn't even care what a near stranger thought about his family. And yet Emery felt like so much more than a random person he'd just met.

A voice deep inside him warned that she could be important. The lightning bolt had struck almost instantly when he first set eyes on her. He'd never put much stock in love at first sight. In fact, he wasn't sure he believed in it at all. A part of him wondered if he just hadn't experienced it before now.

Granted, love was a strong word for what he felt toward Emery. He found himself in unfamiliar territory, a place somewhere in between attraction and something more. Maybe this wasn't the time to put a label on it.

He blew out a sharp breath, smiled and walked over with two fistfuls of coffee. It wasn't lost on him that it felt like the most natural thing in the world to have Emery in his family's kitchen while he brought coffee for them both. "Here you go."

"Thank you." She had her sister's social media page pulled up on the laptop and was studying pictures as she took a mug.

Eli reclaimed his seat beside her. "Do you see anything that stands out in your mind?"

"Sadly, no." She pointed to a picture. "This guy, Chad Markham. I've heard her talk about him from work. He seems to 'like' a lot of her posts which primarily have been about Aria, as expected from a new parent."

"Can't say that I can relate," he admitted. "I never did have one of those pages online."

"Are you kidding me?" Her shocked response made him laugh.

"No. Should I have one?"

Emery shrugged her shoulders. "I just thought everyone was online by now. You know what, though. It's probably for the best that you're not. Don't get me wrong, it's nice to keep up with people but I have like a ridiculous number of acquaintances and not a whole lot of real friends. I don't think I really ever put down roots and it was easy to stay in touch online."

"How many 'friends' do you have?" he asked.

"More than three thousand."

He shook his head. "Who in the world could keep up with that many people?"

"Mine are mostly from the days when I traveled around with a band. I used to date the lead singer." Emery had a past. Eli had a past. And yet hearing about hers still caused a knot of jealousy to form in his stomach.

Rather than go into the details, he said, "Can I ask a question?"

"I'm pretty much an open book at this point."

"Why stay in touch with more people than you can actually have a relationship with?" He'd always been curious about the dynamics and figured his kids would be online someday so he'd better start figuring it out.

"I hardly ever post on my page. The number of people 'friending' me just grew the more famous my ex-boyfriend's band became. Fans of my ex who either met me or saw me with him ended up finding me online and sending a request. It seemed rude not to accept. I keep meaning to prune the list but once I started nursing school on top of working a job and with my sister's pregnancy, I haven't had time." She paused for a second, looking bemused. "Wow. Hearing the details of my life like that make me sound like pretty much the most boring person on the planet." She laughed, and her voice had a musical quality to it.

More of that embarrassment flamed her cheeks and it made her even more beautiful. He liked how easy it was to read Emery's expressions. Every emotion showed on her face.

"Well then, you better put me in that club, too. My usual morning starts at four a.m. and then I work until supper, only stopping to check on my little guys and spend some time with them during the day while they're awake. There's no shame in working hard and trying to improve your life. In fact, the world would be a better place if more people rolled up their sleeves and worked toward a goal."

She practically beamed at him. She wasn't making it any easier to tamp down his attraction to her, especially when her eyes got all glittery when she looked at him. Honey-brown was his new favorite shade.

"Didn't you say all your brothers were moving home or had recently moved home?"

"Yes. All but the youngest, Phoenix, who will get here in the next year or so. In fact," Eli checked the clock on the laptop, "he's probably made it to the hospital by now."

"What kind of jobs do your brothers have?"

"Actually, most of them are coming home to take on their roles here at the ranch. Phoenix is the only one who is staying put in Austin at least until his kid is born."

"Right. You told me that before," she said.

Eli thought about the baby boom that had been happening with his brothers. He took a sip of coffee and smirked.

"What's that all about?" she asked. The break in tension was a nice change. And her curious expression caused his chest to squeeze.

"Nothing. I just wouldn't drink the water around here if I were you."

Aria started fussing, a sure sign it was time for another bottle. Emery started toward the diaper bag.

"I can help with that." Eli was already up and moving toward supplies.

"That would be great. Thank you." Emery picked up the baby instead, realizing how nice it was to have a capable person around and how easy it was to be with someone who saw her as a partner. By the time her last long-term relationship had ended she'd taken on the role of full-time caregiver. It had been easy to slip into that routine on the road when she had nothing but time on her hands. To keep busy, she'd straightened up the tour bus and made sure meals were ready. Volunteering to do it had been one thing until it had come to be expected. Taking care of her ex had become her job.

Emery had happily volunteered to help with Aria, and her sister was always grateful. Haven never seemed to expect Emery to pitch in.

She'd lost count of the number of times Haven had told Emery that having her around was a godsend. Now, she completely understood the sentiment. Trying to do this all alone was almost unthinkable. Being a single parent would have to be one of the most difficult jobs and Emery's respect for them ratcheted up a few more notches.

Eli handed a bottle over to her. She thanked him and soothed the crying baby. If he hadn't shown... Emery couldn't imagine where she'd be right now. She shook off the heavy thoughts and focused on the progress they were making.

At least Haven was in the hospital, getting the care she needed.

As Aria settled, a name from Haven's friend list popped to mind. Emery remembered babysitting for her sister so she could meet up with a guy once...and she remembered exactly who he was.

"My sister kept in touch with an old friend by the name of Brantley Schofield. They met in college. I was looking on her social media page and his picture didn't ring a bell. I've never actually met him but his name sounded familiar. My sister might've mentioned him once or twice over the years. I was on the road for so long and then working or in class. Even when my sister and I talked she always wanted to hear my stories because she said she spent long hours at work and basically had no life. I saw his name and couldn't remember why I recognized it until now. She asked me to watch Aria recently so she could meet up with him."

Aria must've been hungry because she downed the bottle faster than usual and her heavy eyelids closed as she drew in the last of the milk.

"Do you know if your sister and Brantley ever had a romantic relationship?"

Emery shook her head as she burped the baby. "None that she confided in me about, which doesn't mean as much to me now than it would've last month. Plus, she rarely ever talked about him."

She gently patted Aria's back until the gas was released. The little angel went right back to sleep so Emery worked quickly to change her diaper.

Within a few minutes, the baby was sleeping peacefully in her carrier. Emery looked at her niece. What would it be like to sleep so soundly? To know unequivocally that she was so loved and wanted?

Eli's children had it. That unconditional love from their father. It was written all over their innocent smiles. "I'm not trying to change the subject but in case no one's mentioned this to you lately, you're doing a really great job with your children."

A mix of emotion passed behind his eyes. Surprise. Appreciation. Gratitude.

"It means a lot to hear you say that. No one tells you that being a parent is the hardest job you'll ever do and the one you'll most care about getting right. Other than take care of their basic needs of food and shelter, I figure the best thing I can do for them is just to love them for who they are. They're both so different and I love noticing the little things that make them unique." He flashed his eyes at her and her heart stuttered. "It's easy to see how much you love your sister and your niece. I have no doubt that if you decide to have a family that you'll be amazing."

"I'm not so sure about that, but I appreciate the confidence." Emery hadn't given much thought to having her own family, except to say that she wasn't sure she'd ever be ready for one. She'd always liked being able to pick up and go whenever she wanted. Although she could admit that having her niece around was nice. Different, but still wonderful. It felt like a whole new world where she saw everything through the eyes of the little girl.

The changes in her sister had been interesting to watch, too. Don't get her wrong, Haven had always been protective of Emery. It had always been clear to Emery that her sister loved her as both a sibling and in a maternal sense. Haven had been a second mom, considering she'd been the one who'd taken care of

Emery for most of her life. But having Aria seemed to bring a whole new side to Haven alive. And, although Emery had never felt like anything was missing in her life she could admit that having her niece brought a different kind of joy to her life. She'd actually volunteered her days off to help care for Aria. That was saying a lot.

"You make parenting look a lot easier than it is." She put up her hand to stop Eli from arguing her point.

He conceded with a laugh. "I have a lot of help in Marianne and in doing the kind of work that allows me to pop in throughout the day and be with my kids. It's pretty amazing and I realize how fortunate I am. As much as Marianne would never agree, I still need to hire help. She deserves to be in the fun grandmother role instead of a forced daily caretaker."

"Have you looked at her lately?"

"Marianne?"

"Yes. Marianne. There's no mistaking the happiness in her eyes every time she's around your children. I don't exactly think she views them as a burden. In fact, I think she sees it as a privilege to care for them."

Eli stared at the wall for a long moment. "I never really looked at it like that before."

"It's easier for me to see things from a woman's perspective." She laughed. Having grown up with a mother and sister, she was long on understanding women. The opposite sex, however, not so much.

"True enough. Sounds like I need to sit Marianne down and have a conversation with her about how much she'd like to contribute to Oliver and Olivia's care."

"I bet she'd like that. She also might surprise you and say she's pretty happy with the way things are."

"You might be right. I have never seen her happier and she has not once complained about the demands of caring for my littles," he admitted.

"Now that there are other women and children in the house, it seems like if she needs a day off there are plenty of people around to help with that, too."

Eli blinked a couple of times and she'd noticed he did that when he was considering new information. "You have a point there, too. It's good to hear things from a new perspective."

"Any time."

"I hope you mean that." He hesitated before continuing, "When this is all said and done, and I promise you we will figure out what happened to your sister and why, I'd like to stay in touch." This time, she was the one thrown for a loop and her heart started dancing at the suggestion.

Logistically, it was a nightmare but her heart wanted what it wanted and there had to be a way to see each other or stay in contact.

"I'd like that a lot, Eli." Given the extent of her sister's injuries, it might take Haven a while to heal. Without a doubt, Emery would be there for her sister every step of the way. And as much as she appreciated the thought of her and Eli staying in touch, she would take a wait-and-see approach. Besides, he had a full-time job and two little angels in his care. Even so, a tiny burst of hope sprouted wings in her heart that the two of them could find a way to stay in contact. There was something about being in an intense situation and surviving together that stripped away the layers and showed the core of a person. Bonding under these circumstances caused them to get to know each other on a much deeper level and much faster.

"So would I." Eli polished off his cup of coffee. "Do you need anything right now? I'd like to spend a little one-on-one time with my kiddos."

"Is there a more comfortable area of the house for Aria and I? Maybe a place where I could even take a catnap while she sleeps?"

"The two of you can have your own suite. There's a guest room across the hall from mine and the kids' room."

"Well, that sounds almost too good to be true." Pretty much everything about Eli, this ranch and his family seemed fairytale worthy. It should be odd that she felt such a connection to him in such a short amount of time but for reasons her brain had already outlined, it was as natural as breathing.

"Any chance you would be willing to let me borrow this laptop? I'd like to dig around a little more and see if I can come up with anything else with my sister's contacts aside from Brantley. I wish I had his number but maybe I can contact him through social media." She figured it was worth a try.

"Be my guest." He walked over and picked it up, before tucking it under his arm. "May I?" He motioned toward the carrier.

"At least let me take the laptop off your hands." After securing the laptop, she followed Eli upstairs and then down a long hallway. All she could think was that she hoped she could find her way back to the kitchen. "I understand why this place has the word *grand* in its name. I might never find my way back to where we started."

"Follow the hallway. You're bound to bump into someone eventually." Eli shrugged like it was nothing but growing up in a place like this was something else. Again, she was struck by how down-to-earth he was and just how strong the pull toward him had become.

11

Eli spent the rest of the afternoon playing with his children and waiting on updates from his family. He checked on Emery a couple of times, only to find her sleeping peacefully. In fact, she slept through the dinner of meatloaf with a side of mashed potatoes and carrots that he and Marianne had fixed.

"If you want to check on your friend, I'll take the babies for their baths." Marianne's offer was more proof that even though she might not be blood, she was every bit Oliver and Olivia's grandmother. Her offer also reminded him of the conversation he'd had with Emery about needing to have a real sit down with Marianne about her watching the kids.

"That's not necessary. I can bathe the kids. But can

I ask you a question?" He came up next to her at the sink to help with dishes.

"You can ask me anything, Eli. You know that." She rinsed a dish and handed it to him.

"First of all, I can't imagine the last couple of years with Oliver and Olivia without you. Thank you will never begin to cover my gratitude for everything you do for us."

"That's sweet of you to say, but you know I love those kids." She handed him a plate and stopped to gauge his reaction.

"There's no one I trust them with more." She needed to know that. He also needed to give her an out. "But that doesn't mean I'd be offended if you told me that you wanted time for yourself. You have to think about having a little more freedom every once in a while. You wouldn't be human otherwise."

She blushed, and her reaction caught him off guard because it was more like a kid getting caught sneaking a cookie. "What makes you think I need that?"

"I was talking to Emery earlier about needing to hire someone to help out with the kids and she pointed out that you seemed pretty happy doing it."

"She's right. That was very observant of her. She's sharp." She said those last two words with a wink.

He ignored the implication.

"So, are you saying that you don't want me to hire

someone full-time?" Eli needed to hear the words from her.

"I really don't think it's necessary. Between all of us here at the ranch, we have plenty of people to pitch in and help take care of each other. It wouldn't seem right to bring in a stranger to care for our youngest and most precious family members."

Eli didn't point out that his father had done just that when he'd hired her, and it had worked out just fine. Better than fine. He was living proof of how wonderful a decision it had been to bring Marianne into the family.

"You're sure you don't mind? You would tell me if you did. Right?" He searched her face for any hint of hesitation.

"Since when have I ever been shy about telling you what to do, Eli Quinn?" she teased before rinsing a dish and handing it to him.

"I should have asked you before I set out to interview in the past. I'm trying to get better about talking things out instead of thinking that I have to figure out everything for myself all the time."

"You're independent, Eli. That's not a bad thing. And your heart is so big."

"If I am, it's because you made me that way."

"I can't take the credit. You're a good person and an amazing father. I'm proud of you, Eli." He could've sworn he saw water gathering in her eyes when she handed him the next dish. Well, now she was about to turn his eyes into waterworks.

"I like Emery, though." The smile on her face said she'd shifted gears and the twinkle in her eyes said she was up to no good.

"She seems like an okay person." He said it half-joking but his tone came out more serious than he'd intended. "But, I've seen that look in your eye before and—"

"What look?" She handed him a rinsed fork after cutting him off.

"The same one you had when you asked me to pick up a bag of coffee on my way home from the Coffee Bean and Tina Sloan was sitting there waiting."

"That was a coincidence," she argued.

"Coincidence my backside." He countered, not ready to let her off the hook for forcing Tina on him. "She followed me around like a puppy dog every time I went to the feed store after that."

"I only suggested you might be getting coffee around that time. She took the reins and ran with them on that one. I would never have done that to you intentionally."

"Fair point." And yet she could've warned him. She wasn't totally off the hook.

"As for Emery, I didn't say a word." No. She didn't. She didn't have to. Her opinion was written all over the smile plastered on her face.

"She's a friend. I'm just helping her out. That's all there is to it." He needed to change the subject because he wasn't ready to talk about Emery.

"Suit yourself." Marianne said those words so quietly that he almost didn't hear them.

Rather than keep the train on that track, he decided to laugh it off and move on. "I want to put the kids to bed tonight. I'll be gone most of the morning tomorrow on an errand."

"Will Emery and her niece be staying over tonight?" There was no judgment in her voice, just a woman making plans for how many people she could expect at breakfast.

"That's the idea right now. I'm taking her to Fort Worth in the morning. I'm hoping to convince her to leave Aria here for the day if you don't mind another little one hanging around."

"You know that's not a problem for me. The more the merrier as far as I'm concerned. Plus, Oliver and Olivia will enjoy having another baby around." She arched one of her eyebrows. "Madison might be released tomorrow and there could be an important family meeting. It wasn't her water that broke. Turns out, the baby kicked her bladder."

"Yeah? Why do I have the feeling you already know more than you're letting on about that?" There'd be no use trying to pin her down for answers. Plus, he wouldn't do that to her anyway.

Suddenly, the dish she was holding got real interesting to her as she shrugged off his question. "It's not a problem to leave the baby here. She really is a good little girl."

"Uh-huh." He didn't figure she would tell him anything, but no one could fault him for trying. "I'll have to clear it with Emery first. You already know how much I appreciate you. Right?"

"I do." Marianne started humming a familiar tune. It was one that she'd hummed to him and his brothers during their childhood. He loved that his own children were getting to have that same experience and couldn't imagine a better person to care for them.

He reached over and brought Marianne into a hug, kissing her on top of the head. "I hope my father knows how lucky he is to have found you."

Marianne cleared her throat and didn't look up at him. "I'm pretty sure it's the other way around but thank you for saying so."

"I better get those kiddos in the bath." Bath time was one of his favorites of the day. He drew the bath water while the kiddos played with toys in the bathroom. Then, he washed Olivia in her special tub before drying her and putting on her PJs. She went to bed first.

Next up, Oliver. Bath time was his favorite part of the day. Eli loved having a little one-on-one time with each of his kids. He tried to get some special quiet time with each of his children every day. Since Olivia came along and Camille had walked out, alone time with Oliver was in short supply. And that made this time of night the most precious.

After drying off his son and getting him to bed, Eli walked across the hall and then knocked on Emery's door.

"Come in." Her sleepy voice tugged at his heart, not that he needed another reason to be attracted to her.

"I wanted to check on you and see if you're ready for dinner." His first glimpse of her when he entered the room was her black hair splayed across the white pillowcase.

"Food sounds amazing about now." She stretched and then started to get up.

"I got it. No need to rush out of bed." He heard the way those last few words sounded and quickly added, "Not that you *can't* get out of bed." Well, that comment fell into the category of awkward and unnecessary. Eli usually wasn't much of a talker, except he found that he enjoyed talking to Emery. She brought out the chatterbox in him. And, it seemed, the klutz when it came to words.

"If you're offering, who am I to refuse?" Her warm smile put him at ease.

"One dinner coming right up." Eli left the room and was in the kitchen a few minutes later. He checked the baby monitors, relieved to see his angels sleeping peacefully. He heated a container that Marianne had put together for Emery. It was a little odd that there were no voices in the kitchen or people walking around. Now that most of his brothers and their significant others had moved home, he'd gotten used to a full house at all times.

"That was fast." Emery had taken advantage of the extra supplies in the guest bathroom and freshened up. She'd checked on Aria, who was still sleeping peacefully. She'd barely settled with the laptop when Eli brought food that smelled out of this world.

"Marianne is a great cook." He held out the dish.

Emery took the plate and fork, and then took a bite. "You weren't kidding. This meatloaf is so good it makes me want to cry. And these potatoes. What did you put in these?"

"I thought you didn't cry. And the secret is to use sour cream instead of milk." His teasing lightened some of the earlier tension and she managed a genuine smile. It was so easy to be around Eli, unlike the men she'd dated in the past. When it came to her last serious relationship, being with her singer-boyfriend had been like standing in the shadows. With Eli, it felt like her face was aimed toward the sun where she basked in its warmth.

"By the way, I'm impressed that you remembered I don't cry. It's true." Emery decided it was best to refocus on the case and not comparisons of Eli and her ex-boyfriends, none of whom would measure up anyway. "I woke up thinking about my sister's situation. I can't help but think Brantley Schofield might know something about Aria's father."

"Too bad you don't have his number." His voice was a low rumble that traveled all over her body. She took another bite of food trying to distract herself.

"I could send him a direct message on her social media page. That's about the best I can think to do without his phone number." There was no guarantee he would respond and time was the enemy, but it was worth a try.

Eli nodded. He didn't have to be a pro with social media to understand what a direct message was. He sat down on the edge of the bed as she surrendered her plate.

He placed it on the nightstand as she pulled the laptop onto her lap.

Surprisingly, she'd polished off every last bite of food and it was then that she realized how hungry she'd been. She pulled up Brantley's page and sent a message, asking him for his cell number.

Haven hadn't exactly left a playbook when it came to Emery's next steps. She couldn't imagine her sister had intended for the situation to end up like this.

There'd been a couple of rules that Emery had followed. She hadn't gone to law enforcement. Instead, she'd gone into hiding, just like her sister had requested.

There was no length to which Emery wouldn't go to keep Aria safe, and Haven had to realize it. Taking care of the baby had been her sister's number one priority anyway.

Emery wasn't sure what her sister expected outside of those few requests. Emery wondered where her cell phone could be and what her sister could have done with it. For all intents and purposes, it was gone. Honestly, she should feel more stressed out about it than she did. But that probably had more to do with the man in the room than the situation.

With her sister in a coma, the temporary cell phone she'd been given seemed pretty useless. It wasn't like Haven could call with instructions.

Emery logged onto her own social media page, not exactly sure what she expected to find. There wasn't anything out of the ordinary. She hadn't posted on the page in months. She pulled up her email next. Her first thought was that she really needed to go through and unsubscribe to about a dozen retailer sites, considering she had more than six hundred unread messages.

She skimmed through sender's names. There was nothing that jumped out at her. She popped back over to her sister's social media page and sent Brantley a message from there. She didn't exactly pretend to be her sister when she asked for his phone number.

Eli was sitting there, scrolling on his cell phone. Emery decided to check on Aria. The little angel was still sleeping soundly. "Do you think I should wake her up? I'm worried that she may not sleep tonight if I don't."

"Might not be a bad idea." Eli stared at the screen. "I probably need to handle a few work emails. I can take your plate down with me and bring back a fresh bottle."

"Go ahead and take care of your ranch business. I probably need to stretch my legs anyway and I think I remember how to get back down to the kitchen without the need of an escort." She laughed.

Eli glanced up from his phone. Their gazes locked and more of those inconvenient fireworks went off inside her chest.

"I'm not far away if you need me. I'll be across the hall. Just holler," he said.

"Will do." She watched as he got up and walked toward the door. She had to force her gaze away from his muscled back. She knew exactly what she wanted and would have had no qualms about going for it under normal circumstances, but complicated didn't begin to describe this situation.

This time, when she checked the social media page she got a hit. Brantley responded to the message. Since the baby was asleep and Eli was busy, she decided to locate the throwaway phone and call Brantley back, figuring it might not be a bad thing he wouldn't recognize the number.

He answered on the first ring.

"Haven?" It was probably just because Emery had used a number he wasn't used to seeing but she didn't like the surprise in his voice that her sister could be reaching out to him. Then again, this whole situation had her searching for signs of foul play.

"No. Sorry. It's Emery. I'm her sister. I think we met a couple years ago."

"Oh." He didn't bother to hide the shock in his voice. "No. We've never met but I've certainly heard your name before. Still on tour with that...whatever band?"

"Um, no. I'm in school now." Before he could start asking more questions or throw her off track, she started right in. "My sister is tied up right now and she asked me to try to get a hold of you."

"Okay. Haven and I haven't talked in months. I hope everything's okay." She'd bet money on the fact he was lying.

Rather than lie like he just did, she tried to direct the conversation down another route. "She's been trying to reach out to Aria's father. You know my sister had a baby. Right?"

"Yeah. I've been seeing the posts on social media. Is everything okay with the little tyke?"

"Aria? Yeah, she's fine. Great. Beautiful. I thought my sister said the two of you got together a couple of weeks ago, but I must've heard wrong." It wasn't exactly true, but she wanted to gauge when the last time her sister and Brantley met face-to-face.

"Are you sure she was talking about me?" There was something in his voice that she didn't like. Exactly what she couldn't pinpoint. It was the kind of surprise that sounded like the possibility of hearing from Haven again wasn't a good thing. Haven hadn't mentioned that she and Brantley had had a falling out. But then, her sister had been preoccupied with the baby.

So, what was going on? Emery had to consider the possibility that he was surprised because he knew something had happened to her sister. Emery decided to test the waters. "I think so. She's not here right now, but I could have her call you when she gets back."

"That's okay. I'm sure she'll reach out when she wants to talk to me." Also, she realized he'd dodged her earlier question about trying to locate Aria's father. Could he be Aria's father or at the very least know who the man was?

Emery realized just how disconnected she'd been from her sister while she'd been on the road touring. Granted, the two of them had stayed in touch and she liked to believe she'd heard the highlights of Haven's life. But she was seeing just how much she'd missed of the day-to-day.

Now that she had come home and signed up for nursing school, she'd been so busy that she'd talked to her sister even less and almost never about anything that didn't involve pregnancy or Aria.

"Can I ask a personal question?" She figured that she might as well go for it while she still had him on the line.

"Sure." He sounded anything but.

"Are you and my sister in some kind of fight?"

"No. What would make you think that?" he answered quickly. Too quickly. But did that make him guilty?

"I'm probably just reading something into nothing. Never mind."

"Okay." Brantley sounded a little unsettled. "Have her call me. I don't think she has my new number."

"Oh. This is a new number?" It seemed like no one changed numbers anymore. People took their cell phones with them everywhere, including when they moved out of state. So it seemed a little odd that he'd changed his and her sister wouldn't have it.

"Yes. Bad relationship. Long story. It seemed easier to start over with a new number." He issued a sigh, short and impatient.

A bad breakup would explain a need for change.

She could think of others. Running from someone would be a really good reason for a new number. After having her own cell phone taken away this morning by her sister, she also took note that the first thing someone did when they wanted to hide was get rid of their cell phone.

"We've all had one or two of those." She laughed into a deadly quiet line. Her attempt to lighten the mood fell flat. He wasn't having anything to do with her sense of humor or her to be honest.

"Okay. Well then, if you don't need anything else, tell Haven to call."

Before she could respond, he hung up on her.

12

By the time Eli returned, Aria was in need of a bath. Emery didn't want to talk about her unsettling conversation with Brantley while the baby was awake. She wouldn't be able to bring him up without feeling stressed and babies could pick up on the emotions of their caregivers.

"I've never given her a bath on my own before," she admitted to Eli as she patted the baby's back and waited for the gas to clear.

"I can teach you the ropes," he offered.

"I'd like that very much." She thanked him.

Working side-by-side with Eli to take care of Aria wasn't exactly helping tamp down her attraction to the man.

The minute Aria was asleep, Emery updated Eli on her conversation with Brantley.

Eli listened and didn't immediately respond. When he did finally speak, he said, "It doesn't sound to me like he's the father but there's obviously something going on with him."

"Agreed."

"How'd you end the call?" he asked.

"With him telling me to give my sister his new number," she informed him.

"I don't buy the bad breakup excuse." He referred to the reason Brantley had a new number.

"Neither do I," she said.

Quiet sat between them for a few minutes. The air changed with a different energy and her gaze dropped to his thick lips.

Eli seemed to bite back a smile before standing up and walking to the door. Him leaving would be the best call no matter how much her heart protested.

"I told Marianne I'd ask if Aria could stay at the ranch while we head to Fort Worth in the morning."

She started to protest but he cut her off with a hand up.

"Sleep on it before you decide."

Several protests came to mind but ultimately Aria's safety had to come first. She decided to take his advice and see how she felt in the morning.

"Okay," she conceded.

"Good night," was all he said as he closed the door behind him.

Emery drifted in and out of sleep. It was impossible for her to get a really good and REM going, partly because of nerves and partly because of the nap she'd taken.

Tossing and turning enough to twist the sheets beyond fixable, she finally withdrew herself from the covers, and threw on an outfit from the bag she'd packed. She tiptoed out of the room and then made her way downstairs to brew some coffee. Hearing voices drift down the hallway toward her caught her off guard at first. Then, she remembered work at the ranch started at four a.m. Since she didn't want to startle anyone, she cleared her throat before entering the room.

"Good morning. There's fresh coffee." How Eli could basically get no sleep and still sound normal was beyond her.

She returned the greeting and stumbled over to the coffee machine, doing her best to ignore the sensations traveling over her body at hearing Eli's voice first thing.

Fresh mugs were next to the maker, so she grabbed one and filled her cup.

The first cup was the best. The burn on her throat. The strong taste on her tongue.

After a few sips, she felt ready to face the day. She also acknowledged it had been twenty-four hours since she'd seen her sister.

Eli sat at the table talking to the brother she recognized from yesterday as Noah. The pair chatted easily and for a split second she had to choke back emotion threatening to overwhelm her. There was something about seeing the brothers together that reminded her so much of her and Haven. A deep ache sprang up from seemingly out of nowhere, threatening to break her down.

She thought about her sister and then she thought about Aria. Being strong had never been a problem for Emery. But her beloved sister was in the hospital. Feeling helpless was the worst. Not seeing her was the worst.

"You want to join us?" Eli asked, and she welcomed the distraction.

"What time do you want to head out today?" She needed to get to Fort Worth.

"I figured the earlier the better. Most lawyers I know go into work early and we have the best chance of catching them off guard and getting past the receptionist if we're early."

"Then it's probably best if I go get ready."

"What should I tell Marianne about Aria?" Thinking about the possibility of someone staking out her sister's office and a possible repeat of the incident with the truck caused her to lean toward leaving the baby.

These next words were probably the most difficult because nothing in Emery wanted to be separated from her niece right now. But risking Aria's safety made the choice a no-brainer. "I'd like to take her up on her offer."

"She'll be tickled. You've just made her day."

Noah looked up at her. "Have you met Gina and her daughter, Everly?"

"Yes."

"Good. Gina is planning to help out with Oliver and Olivia today so Aria will be in good company." The thought of giving Aria playmates eased some of her apprehension.

"Aria will be in heaven with other babies around." She smiled knowing full well that it didn't reach her eyes. "I better run upstairs and check on her."

Getting out of the kitchen had very little to do with the fact Emery wanted to check on her niece and everything to do with needing a minute to gather herself.

The thought of being separated from Aria caused her chest to squeeze and breathing to hurt. She leaned against the hallway as soon as she was out of sight, closed her eyes, and took in a few deep breaths. She'd read somewhere that deep breathing was supposed to fix everything from stress to physical pain to illness.

Measuring her breaths as she calmed her racing heart, she was startled to open her eyes and see Eli hovering down the hallway.

"I'm sorry. I didn't want to disturb you, but I needed to make sure you were okay."

"I am." There was no enthusiasm in those two words. She was proud of herself for getting them out despite a lack a conviction.

"Is it okay if I come closer?" She appreciated Eli for asking.

"Yes." Her pulse was still erratic and unpredictable as she leaned her back against the wall, hands at her side, palms flat against the white paint.

And then in the next moment, Eli was standing toe-to-toe with her.

Suddenly, his warm and spicy scent filled her senses. Taking in air did nothing more than usher in more of his unique scent.

Need welled inside her body and she knew exactly what she wanted, *needed*. Since he'd given her go-ahead signs, she figured she may as well ask for what she wanted.

"Will you kiss me, Eli?"

He blinked clear blue eyes at her. He took in a sharp breath. And then, he pressed his mouth to hers. He brought his hands up against the wall on either side of her face, leaning into the kiss a little bit more. She teased his lips apart with her tongue before she gently sucked on his bottom lip.

So many sensations rocked her body all at once. She loved the way he tasted, a mix of strong coffee and a hint of the peppermint toothpaste that she recognized from the kind she'd used earlier.

She brought her hands up and tunneled her fingers into his thick black hair, deepening a kiss that had the kind of passion that had been missing her whole life. It reminded her what it was to be alive and feminine and want. It startled her to realize she wanted Eli for more than just one night. Although, she'd take that, too.

Before him, she never believed in love at first sight. This felt a whole lot like it. The intensity of the past twenty-four hours reminded her how fragile life was and that happiness should be grabbed with both hands when it presented itself. And that's exactly what she was doing.

She dropped her hands to his shoulders where she dug her fingers in. Underneath the tips, she could feel his pulse pound in perfect rhythm with hers.

Things were getting heated between them. It was Eli who came to his senses and pulled back first.

"Another time, another place, this wouldn't stop right here." His breath was coming out in rasps.

She waited for the 'but' knowing full well there would be one.

"This is insane because we just met," he continued.

She listened for it, for that one word that turned this scenario down a path she wouldn't like.

"I like you, Emery. More than I probably should admit."

"The feeling is mutual, Eli." More of those butterflies released in her stomach when she locked gazes with him.

She'd never seen so much hunger when another man looked at her. Her breath caught in her throat as her body screamed for more. More of this kind of passion. More of the way he looked at her. More of Eli.

It wasn't until that moment she realized what she had been missing in her past relationships. It was kind of mind blowing to realize what she'd settled for when she finally saw what was possible. The old saying, *You don't know what you're missing,* came to mind. It applied in spades.

"Good to know." There was an unspoken promise in those words. What that promise was would be anyone's guess. Emery had no idea and she was pretty certain Eli didn't know what to do with this 'thing' happening between them any more than she did.

"I can't believe I'm about to admit this to you." She paused, and almost chickened out. But another saying came to mind, *You only live once,* and after the past twenty-four hours she felt like she understood more of what that meant, too. She looked him straight in the eye. "You have the power to hurt me, Eli. Don't do it."

With that, she ducked under his arm and walked toward her bedroom. He didn't follow like she'd half expected him to. On balance, it was probably good. He needed to know where he stood, and more importantly where she stood.

The cards were on the table. It was his play.

Eli stood there in the hallway, thinking how refreshing pure honesty could be. He was fully aware of the leap that Emery had just taken. She deserved nothing less than an honest response from him. Granted, his feelings for her were an out-of-control roller coaster, which made them damn hard to quantify. He'd strapped himself on for the ride without thinking about the potential consequences to Oliver and Olivia.

The crazy thing was he never expected to fall so fast and so hard for someone he barely met despite the closeness he felt. His emotions wanted to argue that Emery was special...and she was. Logic warned that he didn't truly know a person until he'd spent serious time with them...and it was right.

There he stood. Turn his face west, walk down the hallway, and he'd be walking toward Emery. Turn his face east, walk down the hallway, and he'd be heading back into the kitchen.

The kitchen was what he knew.

Emery, on the other hand, was genuine and intelligent. She was so darn beautiful his chest tightened just looking at her. A little voice in the back of his mind piped up to remind him that she loved her family and had expressed Quinn-like loyalty.

If it was just Eli, there was no question he would jump in with both feet. His decisions impacted two sweet, innocent little angels and that would take some thinking on his part. Starting a relationship now when they were so impressionable seemed irresponsible as a parent unless he could guarantee it would go the long haul.

His kids had already lost so much. How could he risk letting it happen again? The question might haunt him until they were grown and gone. And yet, the thought of spending the next fifteen to twenty years without a special person in his life didn't hold a whole lot of appeal, either.

When it came to Emery, another question might haunt him more. What if she was *the one* and he blew it?

"Aria is still sleeping. I'm ready to go whenever you are." Her singsong voice interrupted his thoughts and he realized he'd been standing there the whole time she was gone. Again, he was also reminded that he could get used to hearing her voice first thing.

"Let's do this." He walked over to her and rested his hand at the small of her back as they returned to the kitchen where Marianne had joined Noah. "We're heading out."

Marianne jumped to her feet. First, she walked over to Emery and brought her into an embrace. "Thank you for trusting me with your niece. I hope you won't worry too much while you're gone. I promise to take the best possible care of her. I'll go put a monitor in the guest room right now, so I can see if the baby stirs."

"Thank you for everything." There was so much emotion in Emery's voice and Eli got the feeling her words were short and sweet to avoid getting too choked up.

Emery glanced up at him, and all that emotion was present in her eyes. She didn't speak and he figured there was a good reason for that. Instead, she nodded and he understood that she was ready to go.

Eli walked with her out the front door and to the small parking area in front of Casa Grande. He opened the passenger door of his vehicle and she climbed in. He and Emery chatted easily on the two-and-a-half-hour drive to the law firm, arriving and parking in front of the building at half past seven.

After a deep breath, Emery stepped out of the truck's cab. She tightened her grip on her handbag and led the way through the double glass doors with the firm's name etched in white.

A receptionist's neck and head were all that was visible from the tall reception counter. Hair in a tight bun, she smiled. "How my help you?"

"My sister works here. Her name is Haven Young."

The receptionist's eyes glittered with recognition. "Yes, I can see the resemblance between you two. How's her baby?" Her gaze shifted to Eli and like missile-to-target locked on. Her cheeks flushed and she brought her hand up to her neck.

"Aria is fine. Thank you for asking." Emery's voice was a little sharper than she'd intended but the woman's flirting was unprofessional.

"Is she here?" The receptionist finally took her gaze off Eli and then glanced around Emery. She stood up to get a better view. "She said she was going to bring in the baby for a visit at around six weeks. Is she coming? Has it really been that long?"

"I'm afraid it has. Time needs to slow down, because it's just going by too quickly." Emery tried to throw out something relatable and suppress her desire to block the woman's view of Eli.

The receptionist nodded and gave a knowing look. "Summer is already in full swing and it seems like just yesterday was spring break for my kids." Once again, her eyes locked on their target, Eli. Jealousy sprang up in Emery as she put her hand on the counter to draw the woman's attention back to where it belonged.

"I'm hoping you can help me. I need to speak to one of my sister's coworkers. I forget his name, though. Were you familiar with who she talked to on a regular basis?"

"Oh...no. Not really." Her eyebrow shot up. "You don't know the name of the person you want to speak to?"

"I was out running an errand and thought I would surprise my sister by asking one of her friends to call. She's been a little down since the baby came. I think she misses work and her friends and I thought it might be nice to hear from one of them. I think his name started with an M..."

"We have an attorney with the first name of Mike, but she didn't work in his group. I don't think that's who she was talking about." The receptionist shrugged.

There was no way Emery was leaving empty-handed, not after driving all this way and leaving her niece with the Quinns.

"There has to be someone in her department with a first or last name that started with an M."

"You aren't by chance talking about Chad Markham, are you?" The receptionist's eyes lit up.

The name rang a bell. "Yes. I think that's him." It also hadn't gone unnoticed that the receptionist's gaze had, once again, locked onto Eli. Another shot of jealousy rocketed through her. It was probably the couple of kisses they'd shared that made her feel proprietary toward Eli.

She tapped the counter. "That sounds right."

"I thought so." The receptionist beamed, but most

of her smiles were aimed in Eli's direction. "He and your sister work in the same department and I'm pretty sure I've seen them go out to lunch together. I'll just let him know you're here."

"Thank you." *Chad Markham.* She repeated his name in her mind a few more times. The more she thought about it, that sounded like the right name. Emery repeated his name one more time in her head to cement it there before she turned to Eli. Part of her wanted to see if he realized how much the receptionist was flirting with him. But then a man as gorgeous as him probably got hit on all the time.

Eli took her hand, linking their fingers together and led her to one side of the lobby. "You did great."

Those words of encouragement sent warmth spiraling through her. "At least we got a name."

A set of double doors behind the receptionist desk opened, and a man roughly Haven's age walked out. It wasn't hard to realize that he was looking for Emery and Eli, considering they were the only two in the lobby at this hour.

"You must be Emery." He walked right up to her and offered a handshake. Chad would be considered tall by most standards, coming in at least six feet tall. Eli had a solid four inches on him.

"And this is my friend, Eli."

Chad acknowledged Eli with a quick handshake and small smile.

"What brings you here? Is everything okay with Haven and the baby?" He stood there with his feet six inches apart, shoulders rounded. He had sandy-blond hair and a runner's build. He was a little on the thin side to Emery's thinking.

She motioned toward the seating area. "Mind if we sit?"

She'd been rehearsing what she wanted to ask in the back of her mind since the parking lot. And now, she wanted an extra minute or two to make sure she used the right words.

After the trio took their seats, she leaned forward. "How well do you know my sister?"

"Pretty well. We've been working together on the same team for the past three years and we spent a lot of time together. Why? What's going on?" His eyebrows drew together in confusion.

"She talked about you a lot and that's why I wanted to come here and ask a couple of questions. She hasn't really told me anything but it seems like she's been under duress since the baby was born. I'm thinking that her stress has something to do with Aria's father and I was hoping you could help me out with that." She watched his face for a reaction.

He folded his hands together and studied them. His voice was low when he said, "I never did believe her story about in vitro." He shifted in his seat, clearly nervous about going down this road or breaking a confidence.

"I'm thinking that she's trying to protect the father for some reason. I was wondering if she was seeing anybody from work. Maybe someone who is married even though that doesn't sound like something she would do. You never really know. Right?"

He was nodding his head halfway through her sentence. "She mentioned a name once but I didn't really put two and two together right away. I have no idea why she would be trying to protect this guy, but he's not someone here at work. I don't know if he's married. I saw her with him once and I'm pretty sure he's Aria's father. I'd noticed something different about her, and then he dropped her off one morning. I practically forced her to spill the details. Then, she just stopped talking about him one day. It was like he'd never existed. Has she ever mentioned the name Joshua Beckinsdale to you?"

Emery shook her head. "It doesn't sound familiar. If she mentioned him, she must not have said much because it didn't leave an impression in my mind." She took a mental note of the name, committing it to memory. "Do you remember what he looked like?"

"Tall. Dark. Rich." His eyes widened. "The only reason I remember his name is because a week later I saw him on the society page of the newspaper. I recognized him right away."

"I hate to keep going back to this because it doesn't sound like my sister at all. But, did the newspaper say whether or not he was married?" It was the only reason she could think of that would give him reason to hurt her sister.

"No. I don't think he was."

It would be easy enough to look him up online. A wealthy guy like that would make news. He might also have something to lose if an inconvenient pregnancy showed up.

Eli already had his phone out, scrolling.

"How is your sister doing?" She hasn't been responding to my texts the last couple of days.

"The baby keeps her busy."

"I love her pictures. She's a beautiful little girl." He looked up at Emery and smiled. "I know your sister is so proud of her baby. Tell her to post a new pic. It's been a couple of weeks."

"I will." Emery stood up. "Thanks for telling me about Aria's father."

"Well, I can't be certain it's him. He's my best guess after I did the math." He must've picked up the disappointment in Emery's eyes because he added, "For what it's worth, your sister loves you very much. I'm sure she has good reasons for not telling you about him."

"Thank you." Emery could think of a few. None of which she liked or sounded like Haven. "On another track, did you ever notice my sister having any other friends at the office?"

The sound that came in Chad's mouth was a mix between a laugh and a chortle. "In this place?"

Emery pressed her lips together.

"Your sister is pretty, smart, and a decent person. She wasn't afraid to roll up her sleeves and put in a hard day. Most of the women in the office viewed her as competition either for dating or a promotion. The married women were afraid to let their husbands near her. The single women made it pretty obvious that she wasn't welcome in their circle. Our bosses favored her and I think that made a lot of them jealous."

That explained why her sister never really talked about any female friends from work. It was sad to think that she didn't have any support.

"Look, your sister was the closest thing to perfect we have around here. It rubbed some people the wrong way. That's part of how we became so close. We weren't afraid to build each other up. This place can sometimes be more about tearing others down."

Emery had been in situations like those. Those jobs never lasted with her. She could only imagine how competitive a law firm would be from top to bottom.

"As soon as I see my sister, I'll tell her you're trying to get a hold of her." Emery smiled through the emotion threatening to pull her under. Once again, she thanked Chad and then left.

In the parking lot, she turned to Eli who had been quiet up to this point. "What are you thinking?"

"I know this guy. But not personally. Let's get to the truck and I'll show you something." There was an ominous tone to his voice.

She made a beeline for the vehicle and climbed in the passenger seat.

Last night's conversation with Brantley was still rolling around in her thoughts. Now, they had a new name to work with. Joshua Beckinsdale. The first thing she wanted to do was look up his address and then pay him a visit.

The first real burst of hope took seed in her chest as an important puzzle piece clicked together.

13

"Joshua Beckinsdale is dead."

Eli's statement seemed to knock the wind out of Emery.

"Go ahead and read the rest of the article," he urged her as she stared at his cell phone screen.

The man's death had made front-page news.

"Beckinsdale died of complications following a burst appendix. It was supposed to be routine surgery and has been a shock to his grieving family." Emery blinked at Eli after reading the passage aloud. "He was an only child and sole heir to the Beckinsdale family fortune. The mayor commented on Joshua's death, stating that he was a friend of the family." It seemed to dawn on her who Joshua Beckinsdale was. "No wonder his name seemed familiar. His family helped build half the art scenes in Fort Worth. Their private art collection is worth millions. They have political ties for days, probably having greased more than a few pockets over the years."

Growing up on the ranch, Eli didn't run with that kind of crowd. He had no idea who had money and could care less. Eli couldn't remember a time when anyone at Quinnland spoke about the family's fortune. There, it didn't matter if someone was a ranch hand or heir, everyone worked alongside each other and everyone pulled his or her weight. Being a sole heir could put a lot of weight on a person's shoulders.

"I wonder if this put a target on my sister's back." She blew out a breath.

"It's possible. Did you notice that he was single?" Eli had. There was no mention of Haven or the possibility of her pregnancy.

"That means there's no jealous wife waiting in the wings," she surmised.

"The article mentioned that there wasn't a serious girlfriend, either." It was a bit of information that struck Eli as odd. The reporter had already mentioned that Joshua wasn't married and made another point to mention that he was single. So, it seemed like there was no need to add that there was no serious girlfriend.

"Back to Brantley Schofield then."

"I'm not ready to make the leap just yet. Have you thought about getting a DNA test to prove that Joshua is Aria's father?"

"I can ask my sister about it after she wakes up," she said. He liked the sound of the confidence in her voice.

"If Haven is half as strong as you are, she'll pull through with flying colors." He meant it. Emery had that rare combination of strength, intelligence, and beauty.

The red blush he thought was incredibly sexy turned her cheeks a darker shade of pink. All his protective instincts flared and he wanted to give her answers about her sister.

"I just wish she would wake up and talk," she said.

"There's something I need to say to you and I doubt you're going to like it. I hope you'll hear me out." It needed to be said.

She nodded slowly, cautiously.

"Your sister has been through hell and back. She's healing and that's a good thing. The person who did this to her, however, is getting away with it. I already promised that I wouldn't go behind your back or do anything without your permission. Nothing could make me go back on my word." He paused. "The person who did this to her, who put her in the hospital, is walking around scot-free. It makes my blood boil that your family is dealing with this. Law enforcement can help find the jerk responsible and put the bastard behind bars where he belongs. They'll make faster progress than we will."

"My sister said no law. How do I go behind her back? It's not exactly like I can ask her." The turmoil in her voice was real. Her emotions were raw.

"Let me ask you this. What if the person who put your sister in a coma is after someone else right now? We don't know how big this is—your sister never intended to be in the hospital unable to tell her side of the story and you already told me that she asked you to make sure her daughter was safe."

He was going out on a limb that could backfire. It had to be said. "What if you could stop this from happening to someone else?"

Emery sat there, still. She raked her front teeth over her bottom lip, a sign she was considering his idea.

"I've never gone against my sister's wishes before. I just wish I could've gone to the hospital to see her. I wish she could wake up and tell me what she wants me to do."

Out of the corner of Eli's eye, he caught a vehicle as it creeped through the parking lot of the law office. A truck.

"What kind of vehicle did you say followed you yesterday morning?"

"A truck. Why?" She followed his gaze to the end of the lot.

"Because there's one making its way toward us aisle by aisle. Duck down in the seat. No one knows to look for me." Eli figured if he made a move to leave the parking lot now he would draw attention to himself.

The driver of the truck was looking for someone.

"What's he doing now?" Emery kept low as Eli fiddled with his navigation system.

The truck could pull up behind him, effectively blocking him in. He discretely reached underneath his seat to where he kept a Smith and Wesson in a custom holster. He kept his handgun near to deal with coyotes and wild hogs, even though most of the time he rode horseback, preferring the old school ways of cattle ranching. There were times when it was too wet or rainy to take his horse out.

The truck slowed as it neared. Eli rested his hand on the butt of his gun.

"He's almost here."

Eli went through the motions like he was entering a new destination into his GPS. And then, he started the engine before putting the gearshift in reverse. He had his game face on. Careful not to glance into the rearview longer than a few seconds, he slowly started backing out of his parking space.

A horn blared at him. He put his free arm up and waved in the universal sign for *my bad*.

The truck moved right on past. He reminded Emery to stay down as he backed out of his parking spot and then pulled away in the opposite direction.

One question sat heavy on Eli's mind. *Who called the driver of the truck?*

14

"It's all clear. You can get up now."

Emery's heart pounded against her rib cage as she climbed back in the seat and put on her seat belt. He'd been right before. Haven was a good person. Emery had to believe in her sister. She couldn't possibly have done something illegal. It wasn't in Haven's blood to...hold on a minute. "I've been thinking about what you said a few minutes ago and you're right. We *should* go to the cops and explain the situation. Except that I can't."

"If you agree that going to the law is the right call, why can't you do it?" He really sounded confused now.

"Because of that article. His family has ties to the mayor. Their socialites and very active in politics. I think my sister was telling me not to go to the law *not* because she did something wrong but because the law would lead Joshua's family to us."

"It's possible someone at the law firm recognized you and made the call. It's a pretty high-powered firm," he agreed.

"This feels on the right track, Eli. I know that we're talking about my sister and that makes me pretty biased. I know in my heart that she wouldn't break the law. She is the most straight and narrow person that I know. Between the two of us, I'm the one who is far more likely to go rogue, and I wouldn't do anything worse than drive too fast."

"You think she's hiding Aria from Joshua's family." It wasn't a question.

"That's right. I do," she said. "If you think about it, his family is wealthy and powerful. Their only son just died. I have to think they found something in his personal belongings linking him to my sister, and possibly the baby. He must not have wanted them to know about his child because he kept that a secret, too."

Eli rocked his head as he navigated onto the highway. "It makes sense."

"Why hurt my sister, though? Why not just take her to court and prove her an unfit mother? She's an amazing parent but that wouldn't mean anything to a judge who was in a wealthy family's pocket."

Based on his intense expression, she could tell he

thought she was on to something. She loved the way his forehead wrinkled when he concentrated.

"Powerful people are used to getting their way. It is possible they thought it would be easier to get rid of your sister rather than have to deal with her on a daily basis."

"Are you kidding me right now? I can't even imagine someone so awful..."

"It could be the reason Joshua kept the child from them in the first place. On the outside, he looked like he had a life of privilege. No one ever really knows what goes on behind closed doors with a family."

"Those selfish..." Emery stopped herself right there. A half a dozen choice words came to mind. Spewing more hate would never be the answer. Her conversation with Brantley replayed in her thoughts. He'd seemed uncomfortable and she wondered if the Beckinsdale family had gotten to him in some way. Convinced him to be on their side? Threatened him?

"I could finish that sentence for you, but I won't."

"All I keep thinking is that maybe they got to Brantley. He was acting so strange on the phone, and based on everything my sister has told me about him over the years it didn't sound like the same person."

"What are we going to do about it?" That was the question of the day.

"She told me to take her baby and hide. She knew they were a threat."

"It seems so," he agreed.

"I want to go see my sister." Before he could respond, she held up her hand. "I know it's not possible. But that's what I want."

"How about we find a safe spot, pull over, and then call my security guy for an update?"

"I can live with that for now." She reasoned that Brantley must still care about her sister. He did, after all, respond to her message when he thought it was Haven. That counted for something. "Do you think it's possible to talk to your cousin about the case and get some advice from him?"

"He doesn't have jurisdiction here in Fort Worth. However, he might have a contact he can trust. We won't know if we don't ask."

"True. Maybe after we get the update and then talk to your cousin, we could check on Aria." Her heart hurt for how much she missed her niece. Protective instinct ran deep and she could only imagine how much more so it would be for a mother. "I know she's being well cared for and I can't believe everything your family is doing for us. I just want to hear her little voice for myself even if it is just blowing spit bubbles."

"I understand."

Knowing that an influential family might be gunning for her niece didn't exactly provide a lot of comfort. A family like that would know to cover their tracks. They would have financial means beyond anything Emery could even imagine. If they didn't take her sister out on the streets like gangsters, they'd take her in court. It all seemed so unfair.

Then there was the thought of her sister losing custody of Aria...

Emery couldn't even go there hypothetically. Haven loved her daughter. In fact, Emery had never seen her sister look happier than the day she held her baby in her arms for the first time.

It took a few more minutes for Eli to find an area that he deemed safe enough to park in. He chose a popular Tex-Mex restaurant with a parking lot full of the busy breakfast crowd. The place was hopping.

He chose a spot behind the restaurant in the rear lot. As he backed into a parking spot, she noticed his maneuvering would make it a lot easier to pull out quickly.

There were a dozen trucks parked in the back, lined up just like his so it would be very easy for an eye to skip right over them. She'd checked the sideview mirror multiple times on the way over to make sure no one had followed them and she'd noticed that he'd done the very same thing.

"I'll put the call on Bluetooth so you can hear for yourself." Eli picked up his phone, scrolled through the contacts, and then hit the one marked *security*. She noticed there was no individual name attached.

"How may I help you, sir?" The deep voice sounded all business.

"I have your project's sister in the vehicle with me and we would like to request a health status." Emery wasn't sure she wanted to know why a rancher would need security on autodial. It struck her that Eli was wealthy beyond anything she could imagine. He lived in a world that she could barely fathom despite how down-to-earth he seemed.

"I can only provide an update based on my visuals because her attending physician is unable to release additional information to me personally. However, I can report that the sister is in stable condition, and that her labs looked good on the last go around." Emery probably didn't want to ask how he'd gotten information about Haven's lab work. She figured a professional security firm would have their ways of getting information even in a hospital setting. She also made a mental note to ask Eli if they could investigate the Beckinsdale family.

Could she figure out a way to connect them to her sister?

A phone call beeped in.

"I'll call you right back." Eli clicked over to the other call. "Hey, Noah. What's up?"

Emery's stomach dropped.

Noah's voice came through the speaker. "A couple

is here claiming to be Aria's grandparents. They're demanding to see her."

"No." Emery's tone came out as sharp as she intended. "Under no circumstances do they get to look at her. I don't want them under the same roof let alone in the same room."

"Did they give their names?" Eli asked the basic question that Emery figured she already knew the answer to. It was still good to ask.

"Mr. and Mrs. Beckinsdale. And they're threatening to send a judge if we don't let them see their granddaughter." Noah's confirmation sent a fireball exploding in her chest.

Emery looked to Eli. "How fast can you get us there?"

"Noah. Hold tight. Okay?"

Noah laughed. "T.J.'s on his way home from the hospital. He's so mad he said he could spit fire. He isn't taking too lightly to threats being thrown around on his property and especially ones that involved his family."

"Good." Eli sounded a little surprised. "We're on our way."

"They're still here. Do you really want to confront them?" Eli asked Emery.

There was no question in her mind.

"I want to look those people in the eyes and see for myself what kind of animals would hurt someone else for their own gain."

The several-hours' drive was tense for Emery, and Eli seemed to be deep in his own thoughts for the rest of the ride, too.

Eli pulled into the now-familiar gate, past security, and parked in the lot in front of Casa Grande. He covered her hand with his. "For the record, I think you are incredibly brave and amazing."

"Right back at you, Eli." No hesitation there, either.

"Are you ready to face Joshua's family?"

"I'm more than ready to set the record straight with them," she said.

"Somehow, I don't think you need to hear this from me or anyone else, but you got this."

"That means a lot coming from you. Your confidence in me is everything." She meant it. Emery had always been made of tough material, which didn't mean she never got scared. Words could not adequately express how amazing it felt for someone else to have her back for a change.

Eli leaned across the bench seat and kissed her. She leaned into it, into him.

Without saying another word, they pulled back at the same time and then exited the truck. Hand in hand, they walked through the front door together.

There were voices coming from the kitchen and Emery figured that was the best place to start. She made a beeline for the room in the back of the house.

Glancing around, there were no unfamiliar faces.

"Where are they?" She hoped they were still there because she had a few things she needed to get off her chest and they needed to know just how serious she was about protecting her sister and niece.

"Madison is having her baby." The brother she recognized as Isaac informed them.

"It's early. Is everything okay?" Eli asked his brother.

"So far, so good." Isaac looked to Emery. "Your niece is with Marianne. As is Gina, Everly, Oliver, and Olivia. The people claiming to be Aria's grandparents are in the barn with Dakota, refusing to leave without seeing their granddaughter. T.J. apologized for having to turn around and go back to the hospital. He said he would like for everyone to wait until he returns before we hash this out."

"How did they know where to find us?" Emery asked.

"They didn't say."

Eli linked their fingers and gave an apologetic look. "The truck from the parking lot at the law firm probably took down my tags and traced me back here. I'm sorry, Emery. I led them straight to her."

"Without you, they would've found us hours ago

and I wouldn't have had anyone to trust. We wouldn't even be here without your help." She hoped those words would provide comfort because she meant them. She tugged on Eli's hand. "Is it wrong that I want to go out there and confront them?"

There was so much anger burning through her she could hardly contain it. Hot tears threatened the backs of her eyes, but she refused to cry.

"It's not wrong. It's just not a good idea. We have to play this smart and we will."

He was right and she knew it, but it was hard to stop herself from marching to that barn and letting them know exactly what she thought of them.

Instead, everyone but her and Eli cleared the kitchen and she paced.

15

"The baby came in at eight pounds, three ounces." T.J. walked into the kitchen wearing the widest smile Eli had seen. Being a grandfather looked good on him.

"And Madison?" he immediately asked.

"She's doing amazing." And that's when his father's expression dropped. He walked to Emery and extended a hand. "I'm sorry about what's been happening to your family. I hope you don't mind but Marianne briefed me on the situation. I understand Mr. and Mrs. Beckinsdale are being kept in the barn." He looked Emery in the eyes with the sincerest look. "I don't want to overstep my bounds here, but I hate a bully. I can't say that I've been the man I should've been for most of my life, and I didn't do my wife proud when I lost her, but I'll be damned if anyone pushes around a person close to my family. Would you mind taking a step back on this one and letting me see what I can do?"

Emery's eyes watered, and she seemed to need a minute to gather her emotions. She cleared her throat as though trying to regain control. "I've never known what it's like to have so much acceptance and support. This is what I want for my niece growing up. I'm hugely indebted to your family for stepping up to help my sister and me. The Beckinsdale's have more money than I could ever dream of and political ties I can't even begin to imagine. I don't exactly have any ammunition to go after them with. So, yes, I'll accept all the help I can get. Because my sister is lying in a hospital bed right now and my niece is all I have."

"It would be an honor for me to lend a hand. I know a thing or two about dealing with asshats like these." T.J. winked. "I think we can bring them in the house now."

Eli had never personally witnessed his father throw his weight around. It was easy to forget just how influential the man was. Even though T.J. had shown a softer side of late, make no mistake about the fact his father was a shark.

T.J. fired off a text and in less than a minute a couple close to his age were escorted in through the back door.

Emery had a death grip on Eli's fingers. She tugged

at his hand and then nodded toward Mrs. Beckinsdale, who wore enough foundation to cover bruises on her face. Mr. Beckinsdale seemed to have a violent streak.

Watching T.J. square off with the man was a sight to see indeed. Dakota filed in the back door along with six ranch hands in a show of support for the family.

"I'm not leaving here without her. And I know you realize who I'm talking about." Mr. Beckinsdale was tall by most standards but a solid two inches shorter than T.J.

His wife, by contrast, was a petite woman with a thin frame. Her gaze darted around and Eli couldn't decide if she would hide behind her husband or make a run for enemy lines. Those weary eyes studied Emery.

Emery tugged Eli's hand again. He leaned down and she whispered, "He seems like a real jerk but I can't help but feel sorry for her."

"I was just thinking the same thing."

T.J. folded his arms over his chest and spread his legs in an athletic stance. From the hallway behind, Eli heard footsteps. One by one, five of his brothers surrounded him and Emery.

Mr. Beckinsdale's eyes widened and he seemed to know he was outmatched. And yet, he also seemed determined to figure out a way to come out on top. He took a step forward and poked T.J.'s chest.

All six Quinn sons took an intimidating step forward.

T.J. laughed in the man's face and then waved them off.

"I don't know how things run in the city. I'm a simple man." T.J. took a threatening step toward Mr. Beckinsdale, closing the small gap between them. "But I want you to take a good hard look at everyone standing behind me, and I mean everyone. Better yet, why don't you focus on Emery? Go ahead. Stare at her. Memorize her face." T.J. was in the man's face now. "I don't care how much money you have or how much influence you think you have. You need to know this. You mess with one of us and you mess with *all* of us." T.J.'s words came out like a growl and Eli couldn't be prouder of the man his father was finally growing into.

"That's right." A chorus of men said those words in near-perfect unison.

Mrs. Beckinsdale withdrew her hand from her husband's. She turned on him with a look of betrayal. "Horace, what have you done?"

"I did what had to be done. Don't hurt your pretty little brain trying to catch up now." There was so much venom and hatred in the man's voice, Eli couldn't help but feel a pang of pity for his wife.

"He put my sister in the hospital." Emery stepped forward and T.J. wisely stepped aside. "And now he's trying to take my niece."

"No." Mrs. Beckinsdale drew out the word. The shock and disgust in her voice was evident. She whirled around on her husband. "You hurt an innocent girl?"

Mr. Beckinsdale sneered.

Having a group of men surround her must've given her some bravado because she threw a punch at her husband. "It's bad enough what you've done to me all these years. God knows why I put up with it. But I lost my son. I lost my baby. He didn't want anything to do with you and he hasn't spoken to me in years. And now, I have the chance to do it over again. To do it right this time with my grandchild. I will not let you stand in my way." She turned her gaze to Emery. "I hope you can find it in your heart to forgive me. I swear I didn't know what he was up to and if I had I would've made sure the bastard didn't wake up this morning."

Mr. Beckinsdale whirled around on his wife. "You need to sit the hell down and learn your place."

Emery didn't hesitate. She threw a punch that landed on the man's face. His head snapped back and his nose squirted blood.

She withdrew her fist and shook her hand, wincing even though a small smile tugged at the corners of her lips. Before he could retaliate, T.J. had the man backed up against the wall with his sons and ranch hands surrounding him.

"I'll testify. I know some things he's done, but I

didn't know about this." Mrs. Beckinsdale's voice was shaky but stern.

"That's good enough for me. Someone call Griff." T.J. kept the man pinned against the wall until Griff arrived and arrested him.

Mrs. Beckinsdale sat at the kitchen table sobbing. "I should have known what he was capable of. I can't lose another child. Please, please let me be part of her life."

"Thank you for everything you're willing to do to put your husband behind bars to ensure my sister's safety. It's going to be up to Haven whether or not she wants to forgive you. I'll tell her what you're doing. Until she wakes up and can speak for herself, I can't let you see the baby. I hope you understand."

"I do."

"Do you have somewhere to go?" Emery's concern for the lady touched Eli's heart.

"I've been saving some brochures, thinking about reaching out for help. I was just too afraid of him. But I should've left a long time ago."

"There are services that can help you—"

The older woman waved Emery off. "I've been putting away money for years, figuring he'd leave me at some point. I have more than enough resources to get out of his way and I hope he'll go to prison for a very long time. He deserves it for what he's done."

"Will you give me your phone number, at least?" Emery asked.

The woman's eyes lit up and Eli was proud of Emery. Forgiveness took more courage than holding onto a grudge. It would be a journey and it would take time, but if anyone could do it, she could.

Walking Mrs. Beckinsdale to the front door, Emery gave the older woman a hug. "It will all work out."

There was a hopeful look in her eyes when she said, "I really hope so. I would do anything to have that little girl in my life."

Eli understood the sentiment, but for a different reason. As soon as the door was closed and Emery turned around to him, he realized he couldn't let her go without a fight.

"Emery, I never believed in love at first sight until I met you. I love you. I'm in love with you. And now I know what real love is. Being together is a choice. Staying together is a choice. Finding a way to love each other even on the bad days is a choice." Eli dropped down on one knee. "You need to know, Emery, that I would choose you every day for the rest of my life. It's a little bit crazy because it's all happening so fast, but that doesn't mean it's wrong. I want to spend our lives together, figuring it out. I want to be your family and I want you to be mine. So, what I'm asking is if you'll do me the great honor of becoming my wife."

Eli took in a deep breath and waited for her response.

She brought her hands to his face and he saw tears rolling down her cheeks.

"I fell in love with you almost from the minute we met. At first, I didn't want to believe it was possible because I thought I knew what love was. And then I met you and everything I thought I knew changed. You changed what I expect from a partner, from love." He reached up and thumbed away a tear. "So, yes. I want to marry you. I want to be your family. I choose you, Eli."

Eli stood and kissed his future bride as happiness like he'd never felt before filled his chest. Being with Emery was right.

They broke apart to a round of applause and congratulations. Almost everyone was there in the great hall, including Marianne who was holding Aria.

T.J. stood behind Marianne, his hands on her shoulders. Eli smiled. Everything was right with the world and seeing T.J. and Marianne together was the most natural thing.

With Emery and his entire family around him, Eli had never felt more at home.

16

Beep. Beep. Beep.

The machines in the hospital room beat out a staccato rhythm. Mother and baby were doing well, a relief for everyone after a twenty-six-hour labor and then emergency C-section. Even though Madison was booked in a suite, the room shrank considerably given the sheer number of Quinns crammed inside.

T.J. had seen to it that Emery's sister had been transferred to this hospital. It had only seemed right after what she'd been through. She was on another floor, awake and recovering. It did T.J.'s heart good to be able to help. The man responsible for hurting her was going to prison for the rest of his life, but his wife would be allowed to visit Aria.

He'd requested the meeting that had been

simmering for a while now. It seemed fitting to welcome the newest Quinn into the world, considering the announcement T.J. was about to make. His thoughts drifted to two words, *full circle*.

At one time, it had been impossible to imagine all these faces in the same room with him. Now? Life was good. He was good. No, he was better. He was becoming a better man. And he was grateful for the second chance with his family—a family that would make any man or woman proud.

He cleared his throat, ready to make the announcement everyone had been waiting for. "No doubt you've all witnessed some changes in me over the past few months. We're gathered here today to celebrate a new life coming into the family and maybe a fresh start, as well."

Heads nodded in unison.

"Thank you for showing up when I didn't after we lost your mother." Those words had weighed heavy on his heart and darned if he didn't tear up a little bit while speaking them. Marianne stood by his side, gazing up at him with encouragement and acceptance in her eyes. He had no idea what he'd do without her.

"We know you did the best you could under the circumstances," Eli acknowledged. It was true enough.

The older boys had taken the brunt of T.J.'s anger. It wasn't right, and he would spend the rest of his life trying to make amends.

"Your forgiveness is appreciated more than you could ever know. I realize that it's out of your generosity and not because I deserve it." T.J. put his hand up before anyone could argue. His sons had turned out to be amazing men. He couldn't take the credit.

Marianne grabbed hold of his hand, much to the shock of everyone in the room. Eyes opened, mouths gaping, he figured the cat was out of the bag now.

"My doctor discovered cancer in my thyroid—"

Noises of shock, disbelief interrupted him.

"It's okay. It's all going to be okay. My doctor just confirmed I'm as healthy as a wild horse now."

"Why didn't you tell us?" Noah asked.

"It wasn't because you didn't deserve to know. I wanted to earn your forgiveness, not gain your sympathy if that makes any sense at all."

Again, heads nodded in unison and his heart felt a little more full.

"During this process, I also realized the woman I'm meant to spend the back half of my life with has been right under my nose all along." He turned to Marianne before bending down on one knee. "I love you." He searched her gaze, looking for a sign he should continue. The small smile and tears gathering in her eyes let him know it was okay to keep going. "If you'll have me, I'd like to marry you and spend the rest of my life becoming the man I know I'm capable of being."

Marianne brought her hand up to her mouth. And then she dropped it, leaned forward and laid one heck of a kiss on T.J.

"Yes, I'll marry you. I couldn't love anyone more. You guys have always been my family and I'd be proud to make it official." She beamed and his heart squeezed.

In the background, whoops and hollers filled the room. And joy. It had been a really long time since T.J. had felt a giddy feeling deep in his chest. It had been lost for too long after his wife had died. Now, it was back and he planned to grab hold of the feeling and never let go.

A round of congratulations went up as he shook each son's hand and hugged each of his daughters-in-law. Marianne beamed as she was brought into embrace after embrace. When the two of them had first realized they had real feelings for each other, she'd been worried about telling the boys.

This was happiness. Seeing all the ones he loved smiling and talking, hugging each other and marveling over the new baby.

"While announcements are being doled out," Noah said to a room that quickly hushed. "Mikayla and I have been approved for adoption. It'll take time before we're matched with a child but we just got word it's in motion."

More of those whoops went up. Once talking

settled down again, T.J. figured it was time to make his second announcement.

"There's one more business matter we need to discuss." Everyone quieted. "It's the ranch. I've ridden in the saddle longer than I should. It's time to hand it over or sell."

A collective gasp went up.

"Sell Quinnland?" Eli was the first to speak up.

"You guys can do what you want with it. I'm stepping down and placing it in your capable hands. Each one of you has an equal share. You can run the place as you see fit, sell your shares or decide to walk away altogether." In secret, he hoped they wouldn't. But, it was time to hand over the reins. They could do with it as they pleased.

"I'll have to talk it over with my future wife and my brothers, but I fully intend to keep my share. I want Oliver and Olivia to grow up on the land that I love," Eli said first. His response wasn't unexpected considering he'd stayed on to work the ranch and learn the business. T.J.'s eldest son was fully capable of stepping into his father's shoes.

Noah piped in next, "I'm sticking around. Mikayla and I want to bring our child home to Quinnland."

Other heads nodded in agreement and T.J.'s heart filled with love. He may have messed up his relationships with his kids but he'd given them Quinnland, a home.

As everyone agreed to stay, Marianne stood in the center of the room where she belonged. The smile on her face and the rosy hue to her cheeks—the happiness—were enough for T.J.

When she finally made her way over to him, he took her hand in his and leaned into her ear. "How does me slowing down work on the ranch, spending time with the kids and grandkids, and showing you the world sound to you?"

Marianne looked around, appreciation gleaming in her eyes. "You've already given me the world. All I need is your love."

"That, my darling, is already yours."

***

Are you ready for more exciting suspense featuring Griffin of the Quinn family from USA TODAY Bestselling Author Barb Han? Click here: Texas Cowboy Sheriff

TEXAS COWBOY SHERIFF

CHAPTER ONE

"Good morning, Mrs. Brubaker."

As she spoke, Laurel Roberts immediately crossed the room to the window. She whisked open the floor-length curtains to bathe the room in sunlight. The almost pitch-black room of one of her favorite residents might be good for sleeping, but it was time to rise and shine. Laurel had an unexplained soft spot for the silver-haired occupant in room number seven at Resting Acres, despite Hattie Brubaker's onery side. In fact, Laurel probably liked the centenarian *because* of it.

As Laurel glanced out at the yard, a habit she'd picked up nine months ago after fleeing Chicago, she could have sworn a male figure darted behind a tree trunk. Panic squeezed her chest as she stared out the window, studying the tree, watching for any sign she could trust her eyes, and that her imagination hadn't just gone wild.

Heart racing, gaze focused, she gasped when a gust of wind knocked a few leaves loose. Hand over her mouth, she suppressed a scream. It was fine. This wasn't Chicago. She'd gone to great lengths to ensure there was no trail. He couldn't possibly have found her.

"Are you an angel?" Hattie asked in dramatic fashion after clearing her throat. Laurel gave the tree a last once-over before turning in time to see Hattie make a show of rubbing her eyes like she couldn't believe what she was seeing.

"Nope. Just me. Laurel," she responded, adding quietly, "no one special."

"Come closer, heavenly child. My eyesight isn't what it used to be," the elder resident continued, seemingly unfazed by reality. The woman played the age card better than a World Championship Poker player played Texas Hold 'em.

"I'm right here," Laurel said with a forced smile. The sun was rising on what would be another warm day in early fall. The temperatures in her former hometown had already dipped below freezing. Not here. Texas was just as she remembered, warm and sunny. She would take flip-flops over snow boots this time of year, any day of the week. A change of seasons wasn't due for another week or so in Gunner, Texas, and the short-lived leaf show had yet to begin.

"It's bright out there," Mrs. Brubaker said, pushing up to sitting position.

"Another warm one for the books," Laurel confirmed with a smile. "Can I make you a cup of coffee before I head out?"

Mrs. Brubaker patted the bed. "How much longer until your shift is over?"

Laurel checked her watch. "Technically, I'm done, but there's no way I would walk out of here without saying good morning," she said.

"Sit with an old lady for a few minutes before you go?" Mrs. Brubaker was turning on the puppy dog eyes, making it impossible to say no.

"Of course," Laurel relented, feeling every minute of her ten-hour shift in her aching feet. Mentally, she'd clocked out half an hour ago. But how could she refuse?

"Are you sure you don't want coffee? I don't mind running out for some. The staff lounge is practically right outside your door," Laurel said.

"Well, if it's no trouble," Mrs. Brubaker conceded with a twinkle in her eyes. She loved breaking the rules and this was a huge no-no. Residents had their own kitchenettes, bathroom, and living/bedroom combination. They were supposed to stock their own minifridges and cabinets.

"I'll be back faster than you can put your teeth in," Laurel teased.

"Challenge accepted." The older woman immediately reached for the glass on the nightstand where those pearly whites were soaking.

Laurel continued playing along, hurrying out of the room. It was technically shift change, so the other attendants would be making rounds. As long as the head nurse, a.k.a. Nurse Ratched, didn't catch Laurel, they would be fine. That reminded her. She probably should have grabbed a cup from Mrs. Brubaker's room. Laurel bit back a curse.

She rushed into the lounge, praying Ratched wouldn't be waiting in the hallway. The woman had a sixth sense about these kinds of incidents. She seemed to know exactly when to swoop in and bust attendants for the slightest infraction, and the term 'playful' meant nothing. She excelled at medical care for the residents though, so at least she had that working for her.

This time, Laurel made it back to the room with the contraband coffee without bumping into a soul. This day was starting to look up, if she ignored the creepy-crawly feeling that still lingered after that moment at the window. After a quick visit with Mrs. Brubaker, Laurel would head home to the lake where her kayak would be waiting. Getting out on the water in early November wasn't something she could do without freezing her backside off back home. This was the reason she'd chosen Texas as a place to hide. Plus, she'd never spoken about her time here with anyone up north. The Lone Star State might not be the last place on earth anyone would search for her, but it was close.

"Here you go," she said to a waiting Mrs. Brubaker. "I managed to sneak it out."

The toothy smile staring at her from the bed made Laurel laugh as she handed over the drink.

"Don't get yourself in trouble over me," Mrs. Brubaker said, but the hint of mischief in her eyes said she loved these little games and that she also knew she'd won. This incredible woman had been the first from Texas to swim the English Channel; she'd survived losing two of her three children to Vietnam, and a husband to 'the big C word' as she'd put it; plus, she'd written a physics paper in the nineties that was still being used for core teaching at the University of Texas at Austin. She'd been a spitfire, a real force to be reckoned with, who now spent most of her days sitting at the window reading or looking at pictures of days gone by. Her daughter and granddaughter visited Sundays. They seemed to love her. Laurel had even overheard Ruthie, the daughter, beg her mother to come live with them. Mrs. Brubaker laughed off the request, saying she'd be in the way.

Laurel wanted to ask why, but gathered the subject was touchy.

"Tell me about Chicago this time of year," Mrs. Brubaker said, patting a spot next to her.

"Well, it's cold for one thing," Laurel stated with a visible tremor, before perching on the side of the bed. She'd answered the older woman's question honestly about where she'd come from, praying it wasn't a mistake. The words had slipped out a little too easily, and Laurel had had to remind herself not to be so chatty with people. Impossible with present company, she thought. Lying was hard. Laurel had never developed a gift for deception. "But that's just a preamble for what's to come when the real cold strikes."

"I bet the snow is beautiful, though." There was a wistful quality to Mrs. Brubaker's eyes as she sipped the warm coffee, no doubt wishing she could be on another adventure instead of this bed.

"You won't get any argument from me there," Laurel said. "There is something magical about those tiny white flakes drifting down from the heavens."

Mrs. Brubaker's smile widened at the image.

"My husband couldn't take the cold," she said on a sigh. "Of course, I've always believed anything in the seventies is sweater and coat weather." She laughed and some of the spark returned to her eyes.

A knock at the door interrupted their easy conversation.

"How are you doing today, Ms. B?" Tad Durant asked, stepping inside the room before being given permission to enter. The intern always seemed to pop in whatever room Laurel was in at the end of her ten-hour shift. She bit back a yawn and forced a smile. Technically, Tad had seniority over her. Upsetting him or making him an enemy wouldn't be in her best interest, but she still wished he'd give her some space.

"I'm finer than a frog hair split four ways," Mrs. Brubaker announced proudly as she threw the covers off and swung her feet off the bed. Her flannel nightgown fell well past her knees and Laurel noticed how the older woman had slipped the coffee onto the dresser without Tad batting an eye.

"Good to hear," Tad said. He'd insisted Laurel call him by his first name. She thought it sounded a little too chummy.

"Besides, Laurel is right here if I need anything," the older woman stated.

Tad was just shy of six feet tall with a runner's build. He had dark hair, cobalt blue eyes that seemed to work wonders on the other attendants. His charms didn't have the same effect on Laurel, and she feared it had caused him to double down on his efforts to convince her.

"Speaking of which," he started, turning toward Laurel. "How about we grab a cup of coffee when your shift is over?"

He'd barely delivered his line before firing off a wink. Seriously? All she could think was how badly she wanted to take a shower to scrub off the used car salesman yuck after this conversation with him. Not only was Tad not her typical type, but he gave her the creeps. And, sure, her radar was up despite moving to a town where no one knew her name or background. Laurel had gone to great lengths to ensure no one found her, especially not...

She shivered.

"No, thanks," she said, refocusing on Tad's question. "I'm expected at home."

It wasn't a complete lie. More like stretching the truth to let him down easy. This was the fourth day in a row he'd asked, and this was the fourth time she'd turned him down. Thankfully, she was off the next three days. Maybe by then he would move on to another attendant.

And her kayak was expecting her. Sort of. As much as an inanimate object could wait for someone.

It might have been nine months since she'd left the small suburb on the outskirts of Chicago, but her ordeal had started almost two years prior. The death. The accusation. The harassment. No one wanted to believe she was innocent, or that she'd acted in self-defense. Least of all her ex's family—a family who had money, power, and ties. Soon after the investigation closed and she was deemed a victim rather than a suspect, local cops started harassing her. One in particular made her skin crawl thinking about him and the way he'd backed her up against the wall in her kitchen and threatened to do things to her she'd since blocked from her mind. Ricky Harris. Thinking about him now caused an involuntary shiver to rock her body.

Breathe.

Laurel was confident in the place she'd chosen to hide. Originally from the outskirts of Chicago, she'd headed south the minute she feared her and the lives of the people she loved were in danger after being harassed for a crime she didn't commit.

The small ranching community of Gunner had been a safe haven for the past three months. There was a dozen or so founding ranching families still in the cattle business and then, of course, there was the Quinn family. They were beyond rich. She'd heard good things about their character and had heard there'd been some kind of reckoning with the patriarch. She'd also noticed all attention was on them when one or more of them was in the room. Flying under the radar meant staying as far away from the noteworthy and wealthy Quinn family as much as possible.

Gunner had a small downtown area, complete with an idyllic Main Street. Quaint shops with local flair and eateries lined the streets leading to the town hall. A feed store was at the edge of town; its parking lot was almost always full. Gunner and the surrounding area had many lakes, and that was a very large part of the reason Laurel had chosen this place for her next stop. Harmony Lake had lived up to the promise of its name. Here, time seemed to slow down and Laurel felt like she could breathe again after holding her breath for what felt like an eternity.

The job at Restful Acres had offered a lifeline. The opening had provided the other thing Laurel had needed most, an opportunity to work while most people slept. Then there was Mrs. Brubaker. She had the same hopeful powder blue eyes of Laurel's grandmother.

The incident at Mrs. Brubaker's window still had Laurel's nerves on edge. Just when she was finally starting to relax and believe she might not have to look over her shoulder for the rest of her life, something like that always happened and threw her off-kilter all over again.

Refocusing on the conversation going on between Tad and Mrs. Brubaker, Laurel saw an opportunity to duck out of the room when Tad moved closer to the bed.

She made a show of glancing at her watch as they met at the midpoint of the room. He sidestepped in time to block her view of the door, causing all of her internal alarm bells to sound.

"Look at the time," she said with a shrug, doing her level best to calm her racing pulse and quiet her fight, freeze, or flight instinct.

This time, she wouldn't allow anyone else to have control over her. She squared her shoulders and forced herself to look Tad dead in the eyes.

"Excuse me," she said with a calm she didn't feel. "And if you don't step out of the way soon, I'll move you myself."

Tad's gaze widened in what looked like surprise before he took a dramatic step to the side and swept his hand, as though giving her permission to exit.

It took pretty much all of Laurel's self-control not to comment. Instead, she took a slow breath as she walked past and muttered, *jerk,* just loud enough for him to hear, but studiously ignored his reaction.

"Behave yourself while I'm gone, Mrs. Brubaker," Laurel said with a breezy confidence she didn't own.

"Well, that doesn't sound like any fun," the older woman quipped.

"Then, at least don't get caught," Laurel said. She paused long enough at the door to glance at the bed where Mrs. Brubaker sat. The woman winked and gave a thumbs-up as Tad moved to the foot of the bed. Laurel realized instantly her friend had probably heard the remark. The encouragement gave Laurel another boost of confidence as she headed out the door and toward home.

Laurel admired the way the light reflected off the waves of the lake. The water shimmered underneath the morning sunshine. There was no place that felt as much like home as this cabin despite its small size. The whole place was basically two rooms with a bathroom off to one side, and a laundry nook that was tucked away in a closet hallway. The kitchenette wasn't exactly big family Thanksgiving material, but the space fit her perfectly. She could hear noises from any part of the cabin, so no one would be able to quietly break in the living room while she was sleeping in the bedroom. She'd figured out the first evening that she could leave the door open during a shower and still hear noises in the next room, like if glass broke. She'd asked her landlord to install an alarm, lost the argument. He had agreed to install a deadbolt with a signed year-long lease.

It was a shame that she might have to move again. And it was a crying shame that her time here in Gunner might be coming to an end. Laurel reminded herself not to get too ahead of the game. It was only a possible sighting, she thought as she turned the car engine off after pulling up next to the cabin, unable to shake the neck-hairs-standing-on-end feeling that someone might be watching her. She paused long enough to glance around and saw nothing but inlet, trees, and the cabin directly across the water from hers.

When she really thought about it, anyone could be hiding behind one of those trees.

The inlet opened up at the end of her lane into a massive lake that boaters frequented. She'd used the kayak a couple of times that came with the rental and had made it habit after a ten-hour workday, since it helped her unwind. There was a time when she would have had a glass of wine instead. Not any longer. She needed a clear mind at all times.

Laurel needed to get inside, throw her stuff down, and change clothes. She'd been looking forward to her usual after work kayak ride for the entire ride home. There was no better way to relax after a ten-hour shift than to get out onto the water. But then, she'd always been a water baby. In Chicago, that had meant hot baths. Here, she could get outside much of the year based on the weather patterns.

As she rounded the front of her vehicle, a noise startled her. Her hand immediately came up to her chest as the trash can tipped over, clanking against the brick wall before bouncing off and then landing against the hard soil.

Laurel screamed before her brain could process the fact that it was a cat slinking out, shaking each paw one at a time.

"Henry, I told you not to scare me like that," Laurel fussed at the feral cat that seemed completely nonplussed by her presence. Henry had been her only visitor in the three months since she'd moved into Casa Amarillo, named for its bright yellow decorations.

Taking a moment to will her stress levels down, she breathed in a couple of deep breaths. Then, she started to clean up the mess the little tabby had made.

"What were you after?" she asked, clutching at her heart.

Shake it off, she said to herself. She was seeing shadows where there were none and freaking out over a cat in the trash can. This wasn't the first time Henry had gone foraging for food. It wouldn't be the last. The trash can had banged against the wall in the past while she'd been inside the cabin and it had scared her half to death then too. Every noise still caused her to jump, even if she no longer shrank. Now, when adrenaline surged, she bucked up for a fight.

This also signaled she had probably stayed in the same place for too long and that was truly regrettable.

On a sigh, she picked up the can and scooped up the debris using a flattened cereal box. More critters would get into it, as well as creepy-crawlies, if she didn't get this cleaned up as soon as possible.

"I hope you got something good to eat out of this, sir," she said to Henry. He seemed to have survived the initial shock of the experience as he was sitting on his hindquarters, casually licking his paws. Laurel shook her head. If she was smart, she would stop feeding him. But he needed her, and she had no plans to stop even if the little guy did cause trouble.

The mess was tidied up in a matter of minutes and yet her nerves were probably going to be fried for the rest of the day. All she could think of was getting the kayak on the water and paddling through her tension.

Inside, the cabin had a sofa and two chairs circled around a small fireplace. Having a fireplace at all caused her to scratch her head. It seemed wholly unnecessary in Texas, but, hey, she intended to use it if the temperature dipped below freezing. Cold temperatures happened in Texas. They just didn't stick around. A small round table with a flap down was pushed up against the back of the couch. Three wooden chairs were tucked underneath. Yellow accents brightened up the place and there were the softest, checkered-patterned curtains hanging on the window above the sink.

The duvet on the bed was eggshell white, and there was a bright yellow afghan folded across the bottom. It reminded her of something her beloved grandmother would have made. To Laurel, the owner had missed the mark on the name of the place. He should have named it Casa del Sol, home of the sun.

In a hurry to change into her swimsuit and cover so she could get out onto the lake before the sun scorched, it barely registered when Laurel had grabbed the handle that she realized she'd forgotten to lock the door. Shock seized her. She was getting too comfortable here. Panic gripped her, causing her chest to squeeze and her pulse to skyrocket.

This seemed like a good time to remind herself to breathe. She was already on high alert after the 'incident' with the tree, if she could call it that, and then moments ago with Henry. Then there was Tad, who'd made leaving work stressful. Next shift, she would figure out a way to say hello to Mrs. Brubaker without crossing over with him. She was too easy to figure out. She'd set a pattern, which was exactly against the advice of the private security consultant who'd taken pity on her and given her advice before leaving Chicago. The two of them had gone over her options over an hour lunch, which was all she could afford without knowing where she would be going or how long she would be out of work.

Laurel changed as fast as humanly possible, still trying to shake the 'dark cloud over her head' feeling. Since coming to Gunner, she'd come so close to shedding it like a coat that had grown too small. In the kitchen, she made a quick protein shake and polished it off as quickly as possible. There was something about the routine of coming home, changing, and then having a protein shake before heading out for a morning row after work that was comforting. Anticipation mounted as she thought about the pale blue sky with white puffy clouds that waited outside the door.

The freedom of being on the lake, gliding across the water. The stillness of the lake when there were little to no other people or boats around. Here, she'd been flying under the radar. She'd even managed to avoid the county's sheriff, Griffin Quinn. After being stalked and threatened by a dirty cop, she had no use for either.

Those thoughts were almost enough to start easing the tension that had built up between her shoulder blades and seemed to take up permanent residence since this whole ordeal began. But she didn't want to think about it while the lake called to her. Setting those thoughts aside, she moved outside.

Laurel stretched out her arms as she stepped onto the creaky wooden porch of the rental. She closed and locked the door behind her, double-checking the lock before sliding the key inside the small slit in the waistband of her swim shorts. She pulled her bright yellow kayak behind her as she moved toward the water's edge.

On the shoreline, she didn't even make it to the water when a snake hissed at her. Its head poked out of the grass lining the water, and it came at her. For a split second, Laurel froze. Then, she inched backward a step. She'd been warned about this type of snake from her landlord, but hadn't seen one in the three months since she'd moved in. There'd been spiders and other creepy crawlers, but nothing like this.

It hissed again.

A scream escaped before she could suppress it. A jolt of adrenaline coursed through her veins and she fought against the urge to freeze.

All she could think to do was let out another scream that seemed to carry across the lake and, quite probably, could be heard all the way in Seattle. There had to be some way to scare the snake, that only hissed even more.

Laurel bent down and grabbed an oar while keeping one eye on the snake. All she could think to do in the moment was slap the oar against the hard soil. She must have gotten a whole lot stronger in the past nine months because the oar cracked in half. Her attempt to scare the snake backfired as it launched toward her.

She jumped up and down, smacking what was left of the oar against the earth while screaming bloody murder. Out of the corner of her eye, she caught sight of a fishing boat speeding toward her, no doubt, to the rescue.

The man inside was unmistakable. Sheriff Griffin Quinn.

To keep reading, click here: Texas Cowboy Sheriff

ALSO BY BARB HAN

Don't Mess With Texas Cowboys

Texas Cowboy's Protection

Texas Cowboy Justice

Texas Cowboy's Honor

Texas Cowboy Daddy

Texas Cowboy's Baby

Texas Cowboy's Bride

Texas Cowboy's Family

Texas Cowboy Sheriff

Cowboys of Cattle Cove

Cowboy Reckoning

Cowboy Cover-up

Cowboy Retribution

Cowboy Judgment

Cowboy Conspiracy

Cowboy Rescue

Cowboy Target

Crisis: Cattle Barge

Sudden Setup

Endangered Heiress

Texas Grit

Kidnapped at Christmas

Murder and Mistletoe

Bulletproof Christmas

For more of Barb's books, visit www.BarbHan.com.

ABOUT THE AUTHOR

Barb Han is a USA TODAY and Publisher's Weekly Bestselling Author. Reviewers have called her books "heartfelt" and "exciting."

Barb lives in Texas--her true north--with her adventurous family, a poodle mix and a spunky rescue who is often referred to as a hot mess. She is the proud owner of too many books (if there is such a thing). When not writing, she can be found exploring Manhattan, on a mountain either hiking or skiing depending on the season, or swimming in her own backyard.

Made in the USA
Coppell, TX
10 August 2025